ANGELS &
VISITATIONS

A MISCELLANY

**PORTRAIT OF THE
AUTHOR BY
P. CRAIG RUSSELL**

ANGELS & VISITATIONS

A MISCELLANY
BY
NEIL GAIMAN

ILLUSTRATED BY
BILL SIENKIEWICZ ✛ JILL KARLA SCHWARZ
STEVE BISSETTE ✛ CHARLES VESS
P. CRAIG RUSSELL ✛ RANDY BROECKER
MICHAEL ZULLI

DREAMHAVEN
MINNEAPOLIS, MINNESOTA 1993

ACKNOWLEDGEMENTS

"Introduction" Copyright © 1993 Neil Gaiman. / "The Song of the Audience" Copyright © 1993 Neil Gaiman. / "Chivalry" Copyright © 1992 Neil Gaiman. First appeared in *Grails, Quests, Visitations and Other Ocurrences.* / "Nicholas Was…" Copyright © 1989 Neil Gaiman. First appeared in *Drabble II-Double Century* / "Babycakes" Copyright © 1990 Neil Gaiman. First appeared in *Taboo* 4 / "Troll Bridge" Copyright © 1993 Neil Gaiman. First appeared in *Snow White, Blood Red* "Vampire Sestina" Copyright © 1989 Neil Gaiman. First Published in *Fantasy Tales 2* /"Webs" Copyright © 1990 Neil Gaiman. First appeared in *More Tales from the Forbidden Planet* / "Six to Six" Copyright © 1990 Neil Gaiman. First appeared in *Time Out* / "A Prologue" Copyright © 1989 Neil Gaiman. First appeared in *Soldiers and Scholars* / "Foreign Parts" Copyright © 1990 Neil Gaiman. First appeared in *Words Without Pictures* / "Cold Colours" Copyright © 1990 Neil Gaiman. First appeared in *Midnight Graffiti* /"Luther's Villanelle" Copyright © 1989 Neil Gaiman. First appeared in The Adventures of *Luther Arkwright 10* / "Mouse" Copyright © 1993 Neil Gaiman. First appeared in *Narrow Houses II* "Gumshoe" Copyright © 1989 Punch Publications Ltd. First appeared in *Punch* / "The Case of the Four and Twenty Blackbirds" Copyright © 1984 Neil Gaiman. First appeared in *Knave* / "Virus" Copyright © 1990 Neil Gaiman. First appeared in *Digital Dreams* / "Looking for the Girl" Copyright © 1985 Neil Gaiman. First appeared in *Penthouse* 6 / "Post-Mortem of our Love" Copyright © 1993 Neil Gaiman. / "Being an Experiment Upon Strictly Scientific Lines" Copyright © 1990 Neil Gaiman. First appeared in *20/20* / "We Can Get Them for You Wholesale" Copyright © 1984 Neil Gaiman. First appeared in *Knave* / "The Mystery of Father Brown" Copyright © 1991 Neil Gaiman. First appeared in *100 Great Detectives* / "Murder Mysteries" Copyright © 1992 Neil Gaiman. First appeared in *Midnight Graffiti*

First Edition: October 1993
Sixth Printing: December 2003

Trade Edition 0-9630944-2-4
Limited Edition 0-9630944-3-2

Printed in the United States of America by Sheridan Books, Ann Arbor, Michigan
Book Design by Robert T. Garcia / www.garciapublishingservices.com

Published by
DreamHaven Books
912 West Lake Street, Minneapolis, Minnesota 55408
www.dreamhavenbooks.com
www.neilgaiman.net

CONTENTS

Illustrations

DEDICATION.

For my parents, who taught
me to read, and gave me the
run of the shelves, and who
never minded what I read:
with affection, and with love,
and with gratitude.

The Song of the Audience

Let us call now for the makers of strong images,
Let them come to us now carrying their quills and sharp razors
Let them gash their arms for ink and let them limn.

Look at them tracing their desperation, the makers of strong images
Look at their ink clotting brown and black on the parchment skin
Look: they render us down there limb from limb.

Like dreamers they will reduce us in the rendering,
Like ash and fat to soap we are reduced to our essentials
(Like a shadow who stares at us with eyes of flesh).

Let them entertain us, the makers of strong images.
Let us toss them copper pennies. But let us not forget.
They make the images. We give them flesh.

INTRODUCTION

THIS IS not, strictly speaking, a short-story collection, although you'll find ten short stories in it, stories written over the last ten years. But you'll find other things too: a few poems, a scrap or two of journalism, an essay, a review.

I've spent the last decade writing for a living. I've learned my craft as I've gone about it — indeed, it sometimes occurs to me that when I began I had little talent, merely the conviction that I was a writer, and enough arrogance and hubris to persist. Much — most — of the shorter prose work I did I am content to see forgotten; this book contains the greater part of what's left.

Each of these pieces has something in it or about it that made me want to see it preserved in this miscellany. (Incidentally, the OED defines a miscellany as "literary compositions of various kinds, brought together to form a book".)

I was tempted to rewrite a few of the earlier, clumsier stories, but, in the end, decided not to. It would have been unfair to the author, who was young and sometimes foolish, but had enthusiasm on his side.

I've written a few words — in some cases, a very few words — about each of the pieces here, mostly to do with how and why they were written. You may read them now, or you may begin with the first story, where Mrs Whitaker is already waiting for you.

Chivalry: At the 1991 World Fantasy Convention in Tucson, Ed Kramer asked me for a story for the 1992 World Fantasy Convention souvenir book. He wanted a story with the Holy Grail in it. I told him I'd think about it.

In April 1992, Ed phoned me from the U.S. and told me the deadline was approaching.

I'd been having a bad week. The script I was meant to be writing just wasn't happening, and I'd spent days staring at a blank screen, occasionally writing a word like *The* and staring at it for an hour or so, and then, slowly, letter by letter, I'd delete it and write *And* or *But* instead. Then I'd exit without saving.

So Ed phoned and reminded me that I'd promised him a story. And seeing as nothing else was happening, and that this story was living in the back of my mind, I said sure.

I wrote it in a weekend, a gift from the gods, easy and sweet as anything. Suddenly I was a writer transformed: I laughed in the face of danger and spat on the shoes of writer's block.

Then I sat and stared glumly at a blank screen for another week, because the gods have a sense of humour.

Nicholas Was...: Every Christmas I get cards from artists. They paint them themselves, or draw them. They are things of beauty, monuments to inspired creativity.

Every Christmas I feel insignificant and embarrassed and talentless.

So I wrote this one year; wrote it early for Christmas. Dave McKean calligraphed it elegantly and I sent it out to everyone I could think of. My card.

It's exactly a hundred words long, and first saw print in *Drabble II*, a collection of hundred-word-long short stories.

And while we're on the subject, the first joke I remember learning and telling people, as a very small boy, was a riddle. It went:

> *Q: What do you get if you cross a robin with a vulture?*
> *A: Very depressing Christmas Cards.*

I was younger then.

Babycakes: This was written for an anthology that was a benefit for "Creators for the Ethical Treatment of Animals". It was illustrated by Michael Zulli, who drew the picture of Mrs Whitaker, and Galaad, and Grizzel the horse, that accompanies my story "Chivalry" in this collection.

It's a fable of sorts.

Troll Bridge: This was written for Ellen Datlow, for the anthology *Snow White, Blood Red*, which she edited with Terri Windling. *Snow White, Blood Red* is an anthology of fairy stories, retold for adults.

I picked The Three Billy Goats Gruff.

Vampire Sestina: This is the only piece of vampire fiction I've completed.

John M. "Mike" Ford showed me how to write a sestina. (I owe him thanks not only for that, but also for giving an anagrammatic alternate me the very best song in his delightful novel, *How Much For Just The Planet?*)

It was published in *Fantasy Tales*, and reprinted in *The Mammoth Book of Vampire Stories*, both edited (or co-edited) by Steve Jones, who has edited (or co-edited) more books than anyone else I know, including, with me, a book of nasty poetry for children, called *Now We Are Sick* (published, coincidentally, by DreamHaven Press).

Hi Steve. Hi Mike.

Webs: This is really a science fiction story, although nobody seems to believe that except me. It's set a long time from now.

It was published in 1990 in *More Tales from the Forbidden Planet*, an anthology edited by author and reviewer Roz Kaveney. Rereading it today, for the first time in many years, I noticed odd echoes of Sondheim's *A Little Night Music* and *Pacific Overtures* in there.

Somewhere in my head there's a huge set of linked short stories that tell the story of Lupita; it begins with two wolves guarding a huge old computer in the snow. "Webs" would be about the third or fourth story in the sequence, set fairly early on in Lupita's career.

Six to Six: This is all true, except that the garrulous taxi driver at the end wasn't the one on the way to Victoria, but the one from Gatwick Airport to my house, an hour later.

It was written for *Time Out*, London's weekly listings magazine, for a special issue on London's nightlife.

A Prologue: I met Mary Gentle in 1985, at the Milford SF writers' workshop, but she had a bad cold; met her again in 1986, and we became friends. She also lived in Croydon, one of the very few cities I know my way around, more or less, and I'd stop by and say hello on my way into London. Sometimes Mary would give me rides back from London to Croydon, and we'd have really good literary arguments in the car. Now I think about it, they were more agreements than arguments. But they were fun.

This was the introduction I wrote for her short-story collection *Scholars and Soldiers*. I've written many introductions over the years, but this was really the only one I felt stood alone, and that I wanted to see reprinted.

Foreign Parts: (I wrote an afterword for this story for *Words Without Pictures* in 1989. This is a shortened version of that.)

I wrote this story in 1984, and I did the final draft (a hasty coat of paint and some polyfilla in the nastiest cracks) in 1989. In between those two events it sat in a filing cabinet with a number of other short stories, fragments, things — there's even a children's book in there somewhere — all of them dusty and most of them well forgotten.

This was written and didn't sell — the SF editors didn't like the sex; *Penthouse* and *Knave* editors didn't like the disease. It went into a drawer, only to be pulled out for the Milford SF writers' conference/workshop in 1985. This wasn't the story I took with me to the workshop, which was, rightly, and looking back on it, very graciously, ripped to tiny shreds, but we had some extra time on the Saturday after the five days of intensive lit-crit, and needed some extra stories, and, rather diffidently, I showed them all this one.

They liked it. One of them, British author and anthologist Alex Stewart, liked it an awful lot, and when, about a year later, he signed a contract with New English Library to edit *Arrows of Eros*, an anthology of sex-related SF/Horror stories, he called me and offered it a home.

I said no. Things had changed. In 1984 I had written a story about a venereal disease. The same story seemed to say different things in 1987. The story itself might not have changed, but the landscape around it had altered mightily. I'm talking about AIDS here; and so, whether I had intended it or not, was the story.

If I were going to rewrite the story, I was going to have to take AIDS into account, and I couldn't. It was too big, too unknown, too hard to get a grip on.

But by 1989 the cultural landscape had shifted once more, shifted to the point where I felt, if not comfortable, then less uncomfortable about taking the story out of the cabinet, brushing it down, wiping the smudges off its face, and sending it out to meet the nice people. So when editor Steve Niles asked if I had anything unpublished for his anthology *Words Without Pictures*, I gave him this.

I could say that it's not a story about AIDS. But I'd be lying, at least in part.

On the whole I think it's mostly about loneliness, and identity, and, perhaps, it's about the joys of making your own way in the world.

Cold Colours: I've worked in a number of different media over the years. Sometimes people ask me how I know what medium an idea belongs to.

Mostly they turn up as comics or films or poems or prose or novels or short stories or whatever. You know what you're writing ahead of time.

This, on the other hand, was just an idea. I wanted to say something about those infernal machines, computers, and black magic, and something about the London I observed in the late Eighties — a period of financial excess and moral bankruptcy. It didn't seem to be a short story or a novel, so I tried it as a poem, and it did just fine.

Luther's Villanelle: This was written as a birthday present for Bryan Talbot. (Bryan wrote and drew the *Adventures of Luther Arkwright* comic, which loosely inspired this villanelle.)

The night before Bryan's birthday, on a signing tour in a hotel in Liverpool, Dave McKean and I made a comic of the poem, repeating panels, or types of panels, where lines repeated. I've often wanted to mix formal verse and formal comics. But when it was printed, in a supplement to the comic, two overlays were stuck together, meaning all the lines of verse got tangled up. They're in the right order here.

Mouse: This was written for Pete Crowther's anthology *Narrow Houses II*, an anthology about superstitions. I'd been trying to write him a story about Hollywood, feeding off my experiences in that strange and semi-imaginary place, but found my own dislike of the movie people in my story kept getting in the way — I wasn't enjoying writing it, and would take any excuse to put it off. Eventually, surfing the deadline, I wrote Pete this.

I'm afraid I actually did hear the radio broadcast mentioned in the text.

Gumshoe: The British magazine *Punch* was founded in the 1860s and was a source of amusement (to the English) and of bemusement (to foreigners) for over a century.

Punch was a magazine of humorous articles and stories and cartoons. It was a staple of medical waiting rooms across England. It was also "not as good now as it used to be". This remained true no matter when you began reading or when *now* was. I'd read *Punch* sporadically ever since I was a small boy.

I always wanted to write for *Punch*. I sent the first story I ever wrote to *Punch* (it began with an angel waking a man up, and telling him that he was now in charge of the universe; I remember that much), and received the first nice-rejection-slip of my career.

Punch closed down in, I believe, 1992. Before it went, I had two pieces published in the magazine, both ostensibly book reviews. This is the second of them; the other had a lot more review in it and seemed a bit out of place here. (It also has the true story of my only time on a police identity line-up.)

I also got to go to a Punch Lunch, a hundred-and-thirty-year-old tradition, where a lunch is eaten around the small table on which all *Punch*'s editors, major contributors, and Prince Charles have carved their names or initials.

You may have had the kind of nightmare where you turn up at an exam and realise you don't know anything you're being tested on. They're pretty common. This is a fairly true account of what happened to me when something like that actually happened. The style is one I first saw used by Alan Coren, ex-*Punch* editor and British humorist. It seemed appropriate.

The Case of the Four and Twenty Blackbirds: It's juvenilia, admittedly, but I still have a soft spot for this story. Tidying it for this publication, I found myself changing back a handful of editorial emendations made almost a decade before.

It was the third piece of fiction I wrote to be published in a mass-circulation magazine. (There were two earlier stories, "Featherquest" and "How to Sell The Ponti Bridge", published in *Imagine* magazine. They were good-natured, if uninspired, fantasies, and aren't reprinted here.)

It was also the first thing I ever wrote to be plagiarised. I turned on the television some months after it had been published, and saw it being acted on BBC2 as a sketch on a children's programme. I suppose the writers sensibly assumed that the preteen audience of whatever-the-show-was were unlikely to also read *Knave*.

I remember thinking that I should have been offended, and instead found myself hugely flattered.

Introductions to stories should tell you things like this.

Virus: This was written for David Barrett's computer-fiction anthology, *Digital Dreams*. I don't play many computer games; when I do, I notice they tend to take up areas of my head. Blocks fall, or little men run and jump, behind my eyelids as I go to sleep. Mostly I'd lose, even when playing with my mind. This came from that.

Looking for the Girl: This was commissioned by *Penthouse* for their twentieth anniversary issue, January 1985.

For the previous couple of years I'd been doing interviews for *Penthouse* and *Knave*, two English "skin" magazines — tamer by far than their American equivalents; still, it was an education, all things considered.

I asked a model once if she felt she was being exploited. "Me?" she said. Her name was Marie. "I'm getting well-paid for it, love. And it beats working the night shift in a Bradford biscuit factory. But I'll tell you who's being exploited. All those blokes who buy it. Wanking over me, every month. They're being exploited."

I think this story began with that conversation.

I was satisfied with this story when I wrote it. It was the first fiction I had written that sounded in any way like me and that didn't read like someone else. I was edging towards a style.

To research the story I sat in the *Penthouse* Docklands offices, and thumbed through twenty years' worth of bound magazines. In the first *Penthouse* was my friend Dean Smith. Dean did makeup for *Knave*, and, it turned out, she'd been the very first *Penthouse* Pet of the Year, in 1965. I stole the 1965 Charlotte blurb directly from Dean's blurb, "resurgent individualist" and all. The last I heard, *Penthouse* was hunting for Dean, for their 25th Anniversary celebrations. She'd dropped out of sight. It was in all the newspapers.

It occurred to me, while I was looking at two decades of *Penthouse*s, that *Penthouse* and magazines like it had nothing to do with women, and everything to do with photographs of women.

And that was other place the story began.

I wouldn't write this story now, but I wrote it then. When it was published it was cut by a thousand words; it makes more sense now.

Post-Mortem on Our Love: This is a song lyric, and it's also a riddle of sorts.

It's sung by the Flash Girls, the internationally renowned singing duo consisting of award-winning author Emma Bull, and The Fabulous Lorraine Garland (who set it to music. She said I came to her in a dream and told her what the tune was).

Every now and then I just write things, and they sit in a dusty corner of the computer's hard drive. This was one of them. It sat on the computer for a couple of years, until the Flash Girls asked if I had any spare words.

They sing it very sweetly.

Being an Experiment: This was written for the short-lived British magazine *20/20*, and was commissioned by editor Maria Lexton.

When I was a young journalist-about-town I was a reasonably good drinker, insofar as I remained standing and could form coherent sentences and find my way home again no matter how late I stayed out or how much I drank.

I'm out of practice, however, and have lost the knack; which is perhaps, all things considered, a good thing.

We Can Get Them for You Wholesale: I dozed off one night listening to the radio. When I fell asleep I was listening to a piece on buying in bulk; when I woke up they were talking about hired killers.

That was where this story came from.

I reread it last night, for the first time since its publication in 1984, and realised that it was a John Collier story. Not as good as any good John Collier story, nor written as well as Collier wrote; but it's still a Collier story for all that, and I hadn't noticed that when I was writing it.

Ian Pemble was the editor of *Knave*, where this story and "The Case of The Four And Twenty Blackbirds" (and a third story, "Mss. Found In a Milk Bottle", not reprinted here) first appeared. Ian was a good editor, and a nice man, and an SF fan, and he gave me my first regular journalistic work. It was a monthly interview spot, which paid for my rent, and food, and let me save up for an electric typewriter. During his tenure as editor, *Knave* became, briefly, a good little magazine. He published me, and Kim Newman, and John Grant, and Dave Langford; he commissioned one of Alan Moore's only prose short stories, "Sawdust Memories". He would let me interview anyone I wanted to, as long as we both agreed they were interesting, which meant I got to meet many of the people (mostly authors) I admired or just wanted to meet, and got paid for talking to them. It was a good deal.

(After a few years Ian went back into advertising, and *Knave* began publishing pieces on cars and cardigans and lousy short stories with dull sex in them. They wanted interviews with Sports Stars and Celebrities. It was no longer a magazine I wanted to work for, and so I stopped.)

Father Brown: I do not know whether the first Chesterton book I read was *The Man Who Was Thursday*, *The Napoleon of Notting Hill*, or the collected Father Brown stories. This is because they were all read at roughly the same time — between the ages of nine and twelve, in the little panelled library, upstairs, at Ardingly College Junior School. (The library moved downstairs when I was twelve).

I'd go there whenever I could, and read, pretty indiscriminately. I worked my way through the collected works of J.R.R. Tolkien (actually only the first two books of *Lord of the Rings*, which I read and reread; when I was thirteen I won the school English Prize, and asked for *The Return of the King* as my prize book, so I could find out how it all ended), and H. Rider Haggard, Dennis Wheatley and Leslie Charteris, O. Henry and M. R. James, Col. Oreste Pinto and Baroness Orczy, Anthony Buckeridge and Gerald Durrell and Geoffrey Trease and H. E. Bates and Edgar Wallace and dozens of others — all authors who, in my head, are linked by the faint smell of aromatic pipe-smoke (the library was across from the headmaster's office, and he moved in an atmosphere of Three Nuns pipe tobacco).

G. K. Chesterton was, even then, one of my favourites, and is one of the few authors that I loved as a child I still admire and enjoy, for the hugeness of his fiction, because he could get words to do whatever he wanted them to do, for the colour and poetry and magic.

Maxim Jakubowski ran into me one day in London and asked if I'd like to write an essay for his book *100 Great Detectives*. I could write anything I wanted to about any fictional detective I wanted. "Of course, most of the good ones are already gone," he said, apologetically. "I suppose Father Brown's been taken, then?" "No," he said. "Actually, he hasn't."

So I wrote this for Maxim.

Murder Mysteries: When I had the idea for this story it was called "City of Angels". But around the time I actually began to write it a Broadway show with that title appeared, so when the story was finished I gave it a new name.

It was written for Jessie Horsting at *Midnight Graffiti* magazine, for her paperback anthology, also called *Midnight Graffiti*. Pete Atkins, to whom I faxed draft after draft as I wrote and rewrote it, was invaluable as a sounding board, and a paragon of patience and good humour.

I tried to play fair with the detective part of the story. There are clues everywhere.

There's even one in the title.

This book owes its existence to Greg Ketter, of DreamHaven. Bob Garcia designed it, and had ulcers and headaches and screaming fits on its behalf. Teresa Nielsen Hayden proofread it with persnickety panache. To them; to Michael, Jill, Charles, Craig, Steve and Bill, my friends who did the drawings (not to mention Randy); to Dave McKean, for a most marvellous cover; to the editors over the years who commissioned or accepted the pieces that follow — and to my wife Mary, and my children, Michael and Holly, who mostly left me alone to write them, my thanks.

Sweet dreams.
Neil Gaiman, August 1993.

CHIVALRY

M RS WHITAKER FOUND the Holy Grail; it was under a fur coat.
Every Thursday afternoon Mrs Whitaker walked down to the
post office to collect her pension, even though her legs were no
longer what they were, and on the way back home she would stop in at the
Oxfam Shop and buy herself a little something.

The Oxfam Shop sold old clothes, knickknacks, oddments, bits and
bobs, and large quantities of old paperbacks, all of them donations: second-
hand flotsam, often the house clearances of the dead. All the profits went to
charity.

The shop was staffed by volunteers. The volunteer on duty this afternoon was Marie, seventeen, slightly overweight, and dressed in a baggy
mauve jumper which looked like she had bought it from the shop.

Marie sat by the till with a copy of *Modern Woman* magazine, filling out a
Reveal Your Hidden Personality questionnaire. Every now and then she'd
flip to the back of the magazine, and check the relative points assigned to an
A), B) or C) answer, before making up her mind how she'd respond to the
question.

Mrs Whitaker pottered around the shop.

They still hadn't sold the stuffed cobra, she noted. It had been there for
six months now, gathering dust, glass eyes gazing balefully at the clothes
racks and the cabinet filled with chipped porcelain and chewed toys.

Mrs Whitaker patted its head as she went past.

She picked out a couple of Mills & Boon novels from a bookshelf — *Her
Thundering Soul* and *Her Turbulent Heart,* a shilling each — and gave careful
consideration to the empty bottle of Mateus Rosé with a decorative lamp-
shade on it, before deciding she really didn't have anywhere to put it.

ANGELS AND VISITATIONS

She moved a rather threadbare fur coat, which smelled badly of moth-balls. Underneath it was a walking stick, and a water-stained copy of *Romance and Legend of Chivalry* by A. R. Hope Moncrieff, priced at five pence. Next to the book, on its side, was the Holy Grail. It had a little round paper sticker on the base, and written on it, in felt pen, was the price: 30p.

Mrs Whitaker picked up the dusty silver goblet, and appraised it through her thick spectacles.

"This is nice," she called to Marie.

Marie shrugged.

"It'd look nice on the mantelpiece."

Marie shrugged again.

Mrs Whitaker gave fifty pence to Marie, who gave her ten pence change and a brown paper bag to put the books and the Holy Grail in. Then she went next door to the butcher's and bought herself a nice piece of liver. Then she went home.

The inside of the goblet was thickly coated with a brownish-red dust. Mrs Whitaker washed it out with great care, then left it to soak for an hour in warm water with a dash of vinegar added.

Then she polished it with metal-polish until it gleamed, and she put it on the mantelpiece in her parlour, where it sat between a small, soulful, china basset hound and a photograph of her late husband Henry on the beach at Frinton in 1953.

She had been right: it did look nice.

For dinner that evening she had the liver fried in breadcrumbs, with onions. It was very nice.

The next morning was Friday; on alternate Fridays Mrs Whitaker and Mrs Greenberg would visit each other. Today it was Mrs Greenberg's turn to visit Mrs Whitaker. They sat in the parlour and ate macaroons and drank tea. Mrs Whitaker took one sugar in her tea, but Mrs Greenberg took sweetener, which she always carried in her handbag in a small plastic container.

"That's nice," said Mrs Greenberg, pointing to the Grail. "What is it?"

"It's the Holy Grail," said Mrs Whitaker. "It's the cup that Jesus drunk out of at the Last Supper. Later, at the crucifixion, it caught His precious blood, when the centurion's spear pierced His side."

Mrs Greenberg sniffed. She was small and Jewish and didn't hold with unsanitary things. "I wouldn't know about that," she said, "but it's very nice. Our Myron got one just like that when he won the swimming tournament, only it's got his name on the side."

"Is he still with that nice girl? The hairdresser?"

"Bernice? Oh yes. They're thinking of getting engaged," said Mrs Greenberg.

"That's nice," said Mrs Whitaker. She took another macaroon.

Mrs Greenberg baked her own macaroons and brought them over every alternate Friday: small sweet light-brown biscuits with almonds on top.

They talked about Myron and Bernice, and Mrs Whitaker's nephew Ronald (she had had no children), and about their friend Mrs Perkins who was in hospital with her hip, poor dear.

At midday Mrs Greenberg went home, and Mrs Whitaker made herself cheese on toast for lunch, and after lunch Mrs Whitaker took her pills: the white and the red and two little orange ones.

The doorbell rang.

Mrs Whitaker answered the door. It was a young man with shoulder-length hair so fair it was almost white, wearing gleaming silver armour, with a white surcoat.

"Hello," he said.

"Hello," said Mrs Whitaker.

"I'm on a quest," he said.

"That's nice," said Mrs Whitaker, noncommittally.

"Can I come in?" he asked.

Mrs Whitaker shook her head. "I'm sorry, I don't think so," she said.

"I'm on a quest for the Holy Grail," the young man said. "Is it here?"

"Have you got any identification?" Mrs Whitaker asked. She knew that it was unwise to let unidentified strangers into your home, when you were elderly and living on your own. Handbags get emptied, and worse than that.

The young man went back down the garden path. His horse, a huge grey charger, big as a shire-horse, its head high and its eyes intelligent, was tethered to Mrs Whitaker's garden gate. The knight fumbled in the saddlebag, and returned with a scroll.

It was signed by Arthur, King of All Britons, and charged all persons of whatever rank or station to know that here was Galaad, Knight of the Table Round, and that he was on a Right High and Noble Quest. There was a drawing of the young man below that. It wasn't a bad likeness.

15

Mrs Whitaker nodded. She had been expecting a little card with a photograph on it, but this was far more impressive.

"I suppose you had better come in," she said.

They went into her kitchen. She made Galaad a cup of tea, then she took him into the parlour.

Galaad saw the Grail on her mantelpiece, and dropped to one knee. He put down the tea cup carefully on the russet carpet. A shaft of light came through the net curtains and painted his awed face with golden sunlight and turned his hair into a silver halo.

"It is truly the Sangrail," he said, very quietly. He blinked his pale blue eyes three times, very fast, as if he were blinking back tears.

He lowered his head as if in silent prayer.

Galaad stood up again, and turned to Mrs Whitaker. "Gracious lady, keeper of the Holy of Holies, let me now depart this place with the Blessed Chalice, that my journeyings may be ended and my geas fulfilled."

"Sorry?" said Mrs Whitaker.

Galaad walked over to her and took her old hands in his. "My quest is over," he told her. "The Sangrail is finally within my reach."

Mrs Whitaker pursed her lips. "Can you pick your tea cup and saucer up, please?" she said.

Galaad picked up his tea cup, apologetically.

"No. I don't think so," said Mrs Whitaker. "I rather like it there. It's just right, between the dog and the photograph of my Henry."

"Is it gold you need? Is that it? Lady, I can bring you gold..."

"No," said Mrs Whitaker. "I don't want any gold thank *you*. I'm simply not interested."

She ushered Galaad to the front door. "Nice to meet you," she said.

His horse was leaning its head over her garden fence, nibbling her gladioli. Several of the neighbourhood children were standing on the pavement watching it.

Galaad took some sugar lumps from the saddlebag, and showed the braver of the children how to feed the horse, their hands held flat. The children giggled. One of the older girls stroked the horse's nose.

Galaad swung himself up onto the horse in one fluid movement. Then the horse and the knight trotted off down Hawthorne Crescent.

Mrs Whitaker watched them until they were out of sight, then sighed and went back inside.

The weekend was quiet.

On Saturday Mrs Whitaker took the bus into Maresfield to visit her nephew Ronald, his wife Euphonia, and their daughters, Clarissa and Dillian. She took them a currant cake she had baked herself.

On Sunday morning Mrs Whitaker went to church. Her local church was St James the Less, which was a little more "don't think of this as a church, think of it as a place where like-minded friends hang out and are joyful" than Mrs Whitaker felt entirely comfortable with, but she liked the Vicar, the Reverend Bartholomew, when he wasn't actually playing the guitar.

After the service, she thought about mentioning to him that she had the Holy Grail in her front parlour, but decided against it.

On Monday morning Mrs Whitaker was working in the back garden. She had a small herb garden she was extremely proud of: dill, vervain, mint, rosemary, thyme and a wild expanse of parsley. She was down on her knees, wearing thick green gardening gloves, weeding, and picking out slugs and putting them in a plastic bag.

Mrs Whitaker was very tender-hearted when it came to slugs. She would take them down to the back of her garden, which bordered on the railway line, and throw them over the fence.

She cut some parsley for the salad. There was a cough behind her. Galaad stood there, tall and beautiful, his armour glinting in the morning sun. In his arms he held a long package, wrapped in oiled leather.

"I'm back," he said.

"Hello," said Mrs Whitaker. She stood up, rather slowly, and took off her gardening gloves. "Well," she said, "now you're here, you might as well make yourself useful."

She gave him the plastic bag full of slugs, and told him to tip the slugs out over the back of the fence.

He did.

Then they went into the kitchen.

"Tea? Or lemonade?" she asked.

"Whatever you're having," Galaad said.

Angels and Visitations

Mrs Whitaker took a jug of her homemade lemonade from the fridge and sent Galaad outside to pick a sprig of mint. She selected two tall glasses. She washed the mint carefully and put a few leaves in each glass, then poured the lemonade.

"Is your horse outside?" she asked.

"Oh yes. His name is Grizzel."

"And you've come a long way, I suppose."

"A very long way."

"I see," said Mrs Whitaker. She took a blue plastic basin from under the sink and half-filled it with water. Galaad took it out to Grizzel. He waited while the horse drank, and brought the empty basin back to Mrs Whitaker.

"Now," she said. "I suppose you're still after the Grail."

"Aye, still do I seek the Sangrail," he said. He picked up the leather package from the floor, put it down on her tablecloth and unwrapped it. "For it, I offer you this."

It was a sword, its blade almost four feet long. There were words and symbols traced elegantly along the length of the blade. The hilt was worked in silver and gold, and a large jewel was set in the pommel.

"It's very nice," said Mrs Whitaker, doubtfully.

"This," said Galaad, "is the sword Balmung, forged by Wayland Smith in the dawn times. Its twin is Flamberge. Who wears it is unconquerable in war, and invincible in battle. Who wears it is incapable of a cowardly act or an ignoble one. Set in its pommel is the sardonynx Bircone, which protects its possessor from poison slipped into wine or ale, and from the treachery of friends."

Mrs Whitaker peered at the sword. "It must be very sharp," she said, after a while.

"It can slice a falling hair in twain. Nay, it could slice a sunbeam," said Galaad, proudly.

"Well, then, maybe you ought to put it away," said Mrs Whitaker.

"Don't you want it?" Galaad seemed disappointed.

"No, thank you," said Mrs Whitaker. It occurred to her that her late husband, Henry, would have quite liked it. He would have hung it on the wall in his study next to the stuffed carp he had caught in Scotland, and pointed it out to visitors.

Galaad re-wrapped the oiled leather around the sword Balmung, and tied it up with white cord.

He sat there, disconsolate.

Mrs Whitaker made him some cream cheese and cucumber sandwiches, for the journey back, and wrapped them in greaseproof paper. She gave him an apple for Grizzel. He seemed very pleased with both gifts.

She waved them both good-bye.

That afternoon she took the bus down to the hospital to see Mrs Perkins, who was still in with her hip, poor love. Mrs Whitaker took her some home-made fruit cake, although she had left out the walnuts from the recipe, because Mrs Perkins's teeth weren't what they used to be.

She watched a little television that evening, and had an early night.

On Tuesday, the postman called. Mrs Whitaker was up in the box-room at the top of the house, doing a spot of tidying, and, taking each step slowly and carefully, she didn't make it downstairs in time. The postman had left her a message which said that he'd tried to deliver a packet, but no-one was home.

Mrs Whitaker sighed.

She put the message into her handbag, and went down to the post office.

The package was from her niece Shirelle in Sydney, Australia. It contained photographs of her husband, Wallace, and her two daughters, Dixie and Violet; and a conch shell packed in cotton wool.

Mrs Whitaker had a number of ornamental shells in her bedroom. Her favourite had a view of the Bahamas done on it in enamel. It had been a gift from her sister, Ethel, who had died in 1983.

She put the shell and the photographs in her shopping bag. Then, seeing that she was in the area, she stopped in at the Oxfam shop on her way home.

"Hullo Mrs W.," said Marie.

Mrs Whitaker stared at her. Marie was wearing lipstick (possibly not the best shade for her, nor particularly expertly applied; but, thought Mrs Whitaker, that would come with time), and a rather smart skirt. It was a great improvement.

"Oh. Hello, dear," said Mrs Whitaker.

"There was man in here last week, asking about that thing you bought. The little metal cup thing. I told him where to find you. You don't mind, do you?"

"No, dear," said Mrs Whitaker. "He found me."

"He was really dreamy. Really, really dreamy, " sighed Marie, wistfully. "I could of gone for him.

"And he had a big white horse and all," Marie concluded. She was standing up straighter as well, Mrs Whitaker noted approvingly.

On the bookshelf Mrs Whitaker found a new Mills & Boon novel — *Her Majestic Passion* — although she hadn't yet finished the two she had bought on her last visit.

She picked up the copy of *Romance and Legend of Chivalry*, and opened it. It smelled musty. *Ex Libris Fisher* was neatly handwritten at the top of the first page, in red ink.

She put it down where she had found it.

When she got home, Galaad was waiting for her. He was giving the neighbourhood children rides on Grizzel's back, up and down the street.

"I'm glad you're here," she said. "I've got some cases that need moving."

She showed him up to the box-room in the top of the house. He moved all the old suitcases for her, so she could get to the cupboard at the back.

It was very dusty up there.

She kept him up there most of the afternoon, moving things around while she dusted.

Galaad had a cut on his cheek, and he held one arm a little stiffly.

They talked a little, while she dusted and tidied. Mrs Whitaker told him about her late husband, Henry; and how the life insurance had paid the house off; and how she had all these things but no-one really to leave them to, no-one but Ronald really and his wife only liked modern things. She told him how she had met Henry, during the war, when he was in the A.R.P. and she hadn't closed the kitchen blackout curtains all the way; and about the sixpenny dances they went to in the town; and how they'd gone to London when the war had ended, and she'd had her first drink of wine.

Galaad told Mrs Whitaker about his mother Elaine, who was flighty and no better than she should have been and something of a witch to boot; and his grandfather, King Pelles, who was well-meaning although at best a little vague; and of his youth in the Castle of Bliant on the Joyous Isle; and his father, whom he knew as 'Le Chevalier Mal Fet', who was more or less completely mad, and was in reality Lancelot du Lac, greatest of knights, in disguise and bereft of his wits; and of Galaad's days as a young squire in Camelot.

At five o'clock Mrs Whitaker surveyed the box-room and decided that it met with her approval; then she opened the window so the room could air, and they went downstairs to the kitchen, where she put on the kettle.

Galaad sat down at the kitchen table.

He opened the leather purse at his waist and took out a round white stone. It was about the size of a cricket ball.

"My lady," he said, "This is for you, an you give me the Sangrail."

Mrs Whitaker picked up the stone, which was heavier than it looked, and held it up to the light. It was milkily translucent, and deep inside it flecks of silver glittered and glinted in the late afternoon sunlight. It was warm to the touch.

Then, as she held it, a strange feeling crept over her: deep inside she felt stillness and a sort of peace. *Serenity*: that was the word for it; she felt serene.

Reluctantly she put the stone back in the table.

"It's very nice," she said.

"That is the Philosopher's Stone, which our forefather Noah hung in the Ark to give light when there was no light; it can transform base metals into gold; and it has certain other properties," Galaad told her, proudly. "And that isn't all. There's more. Here." From the leather bag he took an egg, and handed it to her.

It was the size of a goose egg, and was a shiny black colour, mottled with scarlet and white. When Mrs Whitaker touched it the hairs on the back of her neck prickled. Her immediate impression was one of incredible heat and freedom. She heard the crackling of distant fires, and for a fraction of a second she seemed to feel herself far above the world, swooping and diving on wings of flame.

She put the egg down on the table, next to the Philosopher's Stone.

"That is the Egg of the Phoenix," said Galaad. "From far Araby it comes. One day it will hatch out into the Phoenix Bird itself; and when its time comes, the bird will build a nest of flame, lay its egg, and die, to be reborn in flame in a later age of the world."

"I thought that was what it was," said Mrs Whitaker.

"And, last of all, lady," said Galaad, "I have brought you this."

He drew it from his pouch, and gave it to her. It was an apple, apparently carved from a single ruby, on an amber stem.

A little nervously, she picked it up. It was soft to the touch — deceptively so: her fingers bruised it, and ruby-coloured juice from the apple ran down Mrs Whitaker's hand.

The kitchen filled, almost imperceptibly, magically, with the smell of summer fruit, of raspberries and peaches and strawberries and red currants. As if from a great way away she heard distant voices raised in song, and far music on the air.

"It is one of the apples of the Hesperides," said Galaad, quietly. "One bite from it will heal any illness or wound, no matter how deep; a second bite restores youth and beauty; and a third bite is said to grant eternal life."

Mrs Whitaker licked the sticky juice from her hand. It tasted like fine wine.

There was a moment, then, when it all came back to her — how it was to be young: to have a firm, slim body that would do whatever she wanted it to do; to run down a country lane for the simple unladylike joy of running; to have men smile at her just because she was herself and happy about it.

Mrs Whitaker looked at Sir Galaad, most comely of all knights, sitting fair and noble in her small kitchen.

She caught her breath.

"And that's all I have brought for you," said Galaad. "They weren't easy to get, either."

Mrs Whitaker put the ruby fruit down on her kitchen table. She looked at the Philosopher's Stone, and the Egg of the Phoenix, and the Apple of Life.

Then she walked into her parlour and looked at the mantelpiece: at the little china basset hound, and the Holy Grail, and the photograph of her late husband Henry, shirtless, smiling and eating an ice cream in black and white, almost forty years away.

She went back into the kitchen. The kettle had begun to whistle. She poured a little steaming water into the teapot, swirled it around, and poured it out. Then she added two spoonfuls of tea and one for the pot, and poured in the rest of the water. All this she did in silence.

She turned to Galaad then, and she looked at him.

"Put that apple away," she told Galaad, firmly. "You shouldn't offer things like that to old ladies. It isn't proper."

She paused, then. "But I'll take the other two," she continued, after a moment's thought. "They'll look nice on the mantelpiece. And two for one's fair, or I don't know what is."

Galaad beamed. He put the ruby apple into his leather pouch. Then he went down on one knee, and kissed Mrs Whitaker's hand.

"Stop that," said Mrs Whitaker. She poured them both cups of tea, after getting out the very best china, which was only for special occasions.

They sat in silence, drinking their tea.

When they had finished their tea they went into the parlour.

Galaad crossed himself, and picked up the Grail.

Mrs Whitaker arranged the Egg and the Stone where the Grail had been. The Egg kept tipping on one side, and she propped it up against the little china dog.

"They do look very nice," said Mrs Whitaker.

"Yes," agreed Galaad. "They look very nice."

"Can I give you anything to eat before you go back?" she asked.

He shook his head.

"Some fruitcake," she said. "You may not think you want any now, but you'll be glad of it in a few hours' time. And you should probably use the facilities. Now, give me that, and I'll wrap it up for you."

She directed him to the small toilet at the end of the hall, and went into the kitchen, holding the Grail. She had some old Christmas wrapping paper in the pantry, and she wrapped the Grail in it, and tied the package with twine. Then she cut a large slice of fruitcake and put it in a brown paper bag, along with a banana and a slice of processed cheese in silver foil.

Galaad came back from the toilet. She gave him the paper bag, and the Holy Grail. Then she went up on tiptoes and kissed him on the cheek.

"You're a nice boy," she said. "You take care of yourself."

He hugged her, and she shooed him out of the kitchen, and out of the back door, and she shut the door behind him. She poured herself another cup of tea, and cried quietly into a kleenex, while the sound of hoofbeats echoed down Hawthorne Crescent.

On Wednesday Mrs Whitaker stayed in all day.

On Thursday she went down the post office to collect her pension. Then she stopped in at the Oxfam Shop.

The woman on the till was new to her. "Where's Marie?" asked Mrs Whitaker.

The woman on the till, who had blue-rinsed grey hair and blue spectacles that went up into diamante points, shook her head and shrugged her shoulders. "She went off with a young man," she said. "On a horse. Tch. I ask you. I'm meant to be down in the Heathfield shop this afternoon. I had to get my Johnny to run me up here, while we find someone else."

"Oh," said Mrs Whitaker. "Well, it's nice that she's found herself a young man."

"Nice for her, maybe," said the lady on the till, "But some of us were meant to be in Heathfield this afternoon."

On a shelf near the back of the shop Mrs Whitaker found a tarnished old silver container with a long spout. It had been priced at sixty pence, according to the little paper label stuck to the side. It looked a little like a flattened, elongated tea-pot.

She picked out a Mills & Boon novel she hadn't read before. It was called *Her Singular Love*. She took the book and the silver container up to the woman on the till.

"Sixty-five pee, dear," said the woman, picking up the silver object, staring at it. "Funny old thing, isn't it? Came in this morning." It had writing carved along the side in blocky old Chinese characters, and an elegant arching handle. "Some kind of oil can, I suppose."

"No, it's not an oil can," said Mrs Whitaker, who knew exactly what it was. "It's a lamp."

There was a small metal finger-ring, unornamented, tied to the handle of the lamp with brown twine.

"Actually," said Mrs Whitaker, "on second thoughts, I think I'll just have the book."

She paid her five pence for the novel, and put the lamp back where she had found it, in the back of the shop. After all, Mrs Whitaker reflected, as she walked home, it wasn't as if she had anywhere to put it.

NICHOLAS WAS...

older than sin, and his beard could grow no whiter. He wanted to die.

The dwarfish natives of the Arctic caverns did not speak his language, but conversed in their own, twittering tongue, conducted incomprehensible rituals, when they were not actually working in the factories.

Once every year they forced him, sobbing and protesting, into Endless Night. During the journey he would stand near every child in the world, leave one of the dwarves' invisible gifts by its bedside. The children slept, frozen into time.

He envied Prometheus and Loki, Sisyphus and Judas. His punishment was harsher.

Ho.

Ho.

Ho.

BABYCAKES

A FEW YEARS BACK all the animals went away.

We woke up one morning, and they just weren't there any more. They didn't even leave us a note, or say good-bye. We never figured out quite where they'd gone.

We missed them.

Some of us thought that the world had ended, but it hadn't. There just weren't any more animals. No cats or rabbits, no dogs or whales, no fish in the seas, no birds in the skies.

We were all alone.

We didn't know what to do.

We wandered around lost, for a time, and then someone pointed out that just because we didn't have animals any more, that was no reason to change our lives. No reason to change our diets, or to cease testing products that might cause us harm.

After all, there were still babies.

Babies can't talk. They can hardly move. A baby is not a rational, thinking creature.

We made babies.

And we used them.

Some of them we ate. Baby flesh is tender, and succulent.

We flayed their skin, and decorated ourselves in it. Baby leather is soft, and comfortable.

Some of them we tested.

Angels and Visitations

We taped open their eyes, dripped detergents and shampoos in, a drop at a time.

We scarred them, and scalded them. We burnt them. We clamped them and planted electrodes into their brains. We grafted, and we froze, and we irradiated.

The babies breathed our smoke, and the babies' veins flowed with our medicines and drugs, until they stopped breathing, or until their blood ceased to flow.

It was hard, of course, but it was necessary.

No-one could deny that.

With the animals gone, what else could we do?

Some people complained, of course. But then, they always do.

And everything went back to normal.

Only...

Yesterday, all the babies were gone.

We don't know where they went. We didn't even see them go.

We don't know what we're going to do without them.

But we'll think of something. Humans are smart. It's what makes us superior to the animals and the babies.

We'll figure something out.

TROLL-BRIDGE

THEY PULLED UP most of the railway tracks in the early sixties, when I was three or four. They slashed the train services to ribbons. This meant that there was nowhere to go but London, and the little town where I lived became the end of the line.

My earliest reliable memory: eighteen months old, my mother away in hospital having my sister, and my grandmother walking with me down to a bridge and lifting me up to watch the train below, panting and steaming like a black iron dragon.

Over the next few years they lost the last of the steam trains, and with them went the network of railways that joined village to village, town to town.

I didn't know that the trains were going. By the time I was seven they were a thing of the past.

We lived in an old house on the outskirts of the town. The fields opposite were empty and fallow. I used to climb the fence and lie in the shade of a small bulrush patch, and read; or if I were feeling more adventurous I'd explore the grounds of the empty manor beyond the fields. It had a weed-clogged ornamental pond, with a low wooden bridge over it. I never saw any groundsmen or caretakers in my forays through the gardens and woods; and I never attempted to enter the manor. That would have been courting disaster, and besides, it was a matter of faith for me that all empty old houses were haunted.

It is not that I was credulous, simply that I believed in all things dark and dangerous. It was part of my young creed that the night was full of ghosts and witches, hungry and flapping and dressed completely in black.

Angels and Visitations

The converse held reassuringly true: daylight was safe. Daylight was always safe.

A ritual: on the last day of the summer school term, walking home from school, I would remove my shoes and socks and, carrying them in my hands, walk down the stony flinty lane on pink and tender feet. In the summer holiday I would put shoes on only under duress, until school term began once more in September.

When I was seven I discovered the path through the wood. It was summer, hot and bright, and I wandered a long way from home that day.

I was exploring. I went past the manor, its windows boarded up and blind, across the grounds, and through some unfamiliar woods. I scrambled down a steep bank, and I found myself on a shady path that was new to me and overgrown with trees; the light that penetrated the leaves was stained green and gold, and I thought I was in fairyland.

A tiny stream trickled down the side of the path, teeming with tiny, transparent shrimps. I picked them up and watched them jerk and spin on my fingertips. Then I put them back.

I wandered down the path. It was perfectly straight, and overgrown with short grass. From time to time I would find these really terrific rocks: bubbly, melted things, brown and purple and black. If you held them up to the light you could see every colour of the rainbow. I was convinced that they had to be extremely valuable, and stuffed my pockets with them.

I walked and walked down the quiet golden-green corridor, and saw nobody.

I wasn't hungry or thirsty. I just wondered where the path was going. It travelled in a straight line, and was flat, sometimes at the bottom of a ravine, occasionally built up, so I could look down on tree-tops and occasional houses. Valleys, and plateaus, valleys and plateaus. And eventually, in one of the valleys, I came to the bridge.

It was built of clean red brick, a huge curving arch over the path. At the side of the bridge were stone steps cut into the embankment, and, at the top of the steps, a little wooden gate.

I was surprised to see any token of the existence of humanity on my path, which I was by now convinced was a natural formation, like a volcano.

And, with a sense more of curiosity than anything else (I had, after all, walked hundreds of miles, or so I was convinced, and might be *anywhere*), I climbed the stone steps, and went through the gate.

I was nowhere.

The top of the bridge was paved with mud. On each side of it was a meadow. The meadow on my side was a corn-field; the other field was just grass. There were the caked imprints of huge tractor wheels in the dried mud. I walked across the bridge to be sure: no trip-trap, my bare feet were soundless.

Nothing for miles; just fields and corn and trees.

I picked an ear of wheat, and pulled out the sweet grains, peeling them between my fingers, chewing them meditatively.

I realised then that I was getting hungry, and went back down the stairs to the abandoned railway track. It was time to go home. I was not lost; all I needed to do was follow my path home once more.

There was a troll waiting for me, under the bridge.

"I'm a troll," he said. Then he paused, and added, more or less as an afterthought, "Fol rol de ol rol."

He was huge: his head brushed the top of the brick arch. He was more or less translucent: I could see the bricks and trees behind him, dimmed but not lost. He was all my nightmares given flesh. He had huge strong teeth, and rending claws, and strong, hairy hands. His hair was long, like one of my sister's little plastic gonks, and his eyes bulged. He was naked, and his penis hung from the bush of gonk hair between his legs.

"I heard you, Jack," he whispered, in a voice like the wind. "I heard you trip-trapping over my bridge. And now I'm going to eat your life."

I was only seven, but it was daylight, and I do not remember being scared. It is good for children to find themselves facing the elements of a fairy tale — they are well-equipped to deal with these.

"Don't eat me," I said to the troll. I was wearing a stripy brown T-shirt, and brown corduroy trousers. My hair also was brown, and I was missing a front tooth. I was learning to whistle between my teeth, but wasn't there yet.

"I'm going to eat your life, Jack," said the troll.

I stared the troll in the face. "My big sister is going to be coming down the path soon," I lied, "and she's far tastier than me. Eat her instead."

31

The troll sniffed the air, and smiled. "You're all alone," he said. "There's nothing else on the path. Nothing at all." Then he leaned down, and ran his fingers over me: it felt like butterflies were brushing my face — like the touch of a blind person. Then he snuffled his fingers, and shook his huge head. "You don't have a big sister. You've only a younger sister, and she's at her friend's today."

"Can you tell all that from smell?" I asked, amazed.

"Trolls can smell the rainbows, trolls can smell the stars," it whispered sadly. "Trolls can smell the dreams you dreamed before you were ever born. Come close to me and I'll eat your life."

"I've got precious stones in my pocket," I told the troll. "Take them, not me. Look." I showed him the lava jewel rocks I had found earlier.

"Clinker," said the troll. "The discarded refuse of steam trains. Of no value to me."

He opened his mouth wide. Sharp teeth. Breath that smelled of leaf mould and the underneaths of things. "Eat. Now."

He became more and more solid to me, more and more real; and the world outside became flatter, began to fade.

"Wait." I dug my feet into the damp earth beneath the bridge, wiggled my toes, held on tightly to the real world. I stared into his big eyes. "You don't want to eat my life. Not yet. I — I'm only seven. I haven't *lived* at all yet. There are books I haven't read yet. I've never been on an aeroplane. I can't whistle yet — not really. Why don't you let me go? When I'm older and bigger and more of a meal I'll come back to you."

The troll stared at me with eyes like headlamps.

Then it nodded.

"When you come back, then," it said. And it smiled.

I turned around and walked back down the silent straight path where the railway lines had once been.

After a while I began to run.

I pounded down the track in the green light, puffing and blowing, until I felt a stabbing ache beneath my ribcage, the pain of stitch; and, clutching my side, I stumbled home.

§ § §

The fields started to go, as I grew older. One by one, row by row, houses sprang up with roads named after wildflowers and respectable authors. Our home — an aging, tattered Victorian house — was sold, and torn down; new houses covered the garden.

They built houses everywhere.

I once got lost in the new housing estate that covered two meadows I had once known every inch of. I didn't mind too much that the fields were going, though. The old manor house was bought by a multinational, and the grounds became more houses.

It was eight years before I returned to the old railway line, and when I did, I was not alone.

I was fifteen; I'd changed schools twice in that time. Her name was Louise, and she was my first love.

I loved her grey eyes, and her fine light brown hair, and her gawky way of walking (like a fawn just learning to walk which sounds really dumb, for which I apologise): I saw her chewing gum, when I was thirteen, and I fell for her like a suicide from a bridge.

The main trouble with being in love with Louise was that we were best friends, and we were both going out with other people.

I'd never told her I loved her, or even that I fancied her. We were buddies.

I'd been at her house that evening: we sat in her room and played *Rattus Norvegicus*, the first Stranglers LP; it was the beginning of punk, and everything seemed so exciting: the possibilities, in music as in everything else, were endless. Eventually it was time for me to go home, and she decided to accompany me. We held hands, innocently, just pals, and we strolled the ten-minute walk to my house.

The moon was bright, and the world was visible and colourless, and the night was warm.

We got to my house. Saw the lights inside, and stood in the driveway, and talked about the band I was starting. We didn't go in.

Then it was decided that I'd walk *her* home. So we walked back to her house.

Angels and Visitations

She told me about the battles she was having with her younger sister, who was stealing her make-up and perfume. Louise suspected that her sister was having sex with boys. Louise was a virgin. We both were.

We stood in the road outside her house, under the sodium-yellow street-light, and we stared at each other's black lips and pale yellow faces.

We grinned at each other.

Then we just walked, picking quiet roads and empty paths. In one of the new housing estates a path led us into the woodland, and we followed it.

The path was straight and dark; but the lights of distant houses shone like stars on the ground, and the moon gave us enough light to see. Once we were scared, when something snuffled and snorted in front of us. We pressed close, saw it was a badger, laughed and hugged and kept on walking.

We talked quiet nonsense about what we dreamed and wanted and thought.

And all the time I wanted to kiss her and feel her breasts, and maybe put my hand between her legs.

Finally I saw my chance. There was an old brick bridge over the path, and we stopped beneath it. I pressed up against her. Her mouth opened against mine.

Then she went cold and stiff, and stopped moving.

"Hello," said the troll.

I let go of Louise. It was dark beneath the bridge, but the shape of the troll filled the darkness.

"I froze her," said the troll, "so we can talk. Now: I'm going to eat your life."

My heart pounded, and I could feel myself trembling.

"No."

"You said you'd come back to me. And you have. Did you learn to whistle?"

"Yes."

"That's good. I never could whistle." It sniffed, and nodded. "I am pleased. You have grown in life and experience. More to eat. More for me."

I grabbed Louise, a taut zombie, and pushed her forward. "Don't take me. I don't want to die. Take *her*. I bet she's much tastier than me. And she's two months older than I am. Why don't you take her?"

The troll was silent.

It sniffed Louise from toe to head, snuffling at her feet and crotch and breasts and hair.

Then it looked at me.

"She's an innocent," it said. "You're not. I don't want her. I want you."

I walked to the opening of the bridge and stared up at the stars in the night.

"But there's so much I've never done," I said, partly to myself. "I mean, I've never. Well, I've never had sex. And I've never been to America. I haven't..." I paused. " I haven't *done* anything. Not yet."

The troll said nothing.

"I could come back to you. When I'm older."

The troll said nothing.

"I *will* come back. Honest I will."

"Come back to me?" said Louise. "Why? Where are you going?"

I turned around. The troll had gone, and the girl I had thought I loved was standing in the shadows beneath the bridge.

"We're going home," I told her. "Come on."

We walked back, and never said anything.

She went out with the drummer in the punk band I started, and, much later, married someone else. We met once, on a train, after she was married, and she asked me if I remembered that night.

I said I did.

"I really liked you, that night, Jack," she told me. "I thought you were going to kiss me. I thought you were going to ask me out. I would have said yes. If you had."

"But I didn't."

"No," she said. "You didn't." Her hair was cut very short. It didn't suit her.

I never saw her again. The trim woman with the taut smile was not the girl I had loved, and talking to her made me feel uncomfortable.

§　§　§

Angels and Visitations

I moved to London, and then, some years later, I moved back again, but the town I returned to was not the town I remembered: there were no fields, no farms, no little flint lanes; and I moved away as soon as I could, to a tiny village, ten miles down the road.

I moved with my family — I was married by now, with a toddler — into an old house that had once, many years before, been a railway station. The tracks had been dug up, and the old couple who lived opposite us used it to grow vegetables.

I was getting older. One day I found a grey hair; on another, I heard a recording of myself talking, and I realised I sounded just like my father.

I was working in London, doing A & R for one of the major record companies. I was commuting into London by train most days, coming back some evenings.

I had to keep a small flat in London; it's hard to commute when the bands you're checking out don't even stagger onto the stage until midnight. It also meant that it was fairly easy to get laid, if I wanted to, which I did.

I thought that Eleanora — that was my wife's name; I should have mentioned that before, I suppose — didn't know about the other women; but I got back from a two-week jaunt to New York one winter's day, and I when I arrived at the house it was empty and cold.

She had left a letter, not a note. Fifteen pages, neatly typed, and every word of it was true. Including the PS, which read: *You really don't love me. And you never did.*

I put on a heavy coat, and I left the house and just walked, stunned and slightly numb.

There was no snow on the ground, but there was a hard frost, and the leaves crunched under my feet as I walked. The trees were skeletal black against the harsh grey winter sky.

I walked down the side of the road. Cars passed me, travelling to and from London. Once I tripped on a branch, half hidden in a heap of brown leaves, ripping my trousers, cutting my leg.

I reached the next village. There was a river at right angles to the road, and a path I'd never seen before beside it, and I walked down the path, and stared at the river, partly frozen. It gurgled and plashed and sang.

The path led off through fields; it was straight and grassy.

I found a rock, half buried, on one side of the path. I picked it up, brushed off the mud. It was a melted lump of purplish stuff, with a strange rainbow sheen to it. I put it into the pocket of my coat and held it in my hand as I walked, its presence warm and reassuring.

The river meandered away across the fields, and I walked on in silence.

I had walked for an hour before I saw houses — new, and small and square — on the embankment above me.

And then I saw the bridge, and I knew where I was: I was on the old railway path, and I'd been coming down it from the other direction.

There were graffiti painted on the side of the bridge: *Fuck* and *Barry Loves Susan* and the omnipresent *NF* of the National Front.

I stood beneath the bridge, in the red brick arch, stood among the ice cream wrappers, and the crisp packets and the single, sad, used condom, and watched my breath steam in the cold afternoon air.

The blood had dried into my trousers.

Cars passed over the bridge above me; I could hear a radio playing loudly in one of them.

"Hello?" I said, quietly, feeling embarrassed, feeling foolish. "Hello?"

There was no answer. The wind rustled the crisp packets and the leaves.

"I came back. I said I would. And I did. Hello?"

Silence.

I began to cry then, stupidly, silently, sobbing under the bridge.

A hand touched my face, and I looked up.

"I didn't think you'd come back," said the troll.

He was my height now, but otherwise unchanged. His long gonk hair was unkempt and had leaves in it, and his eyes were wide and lonely.

I shrugged, then wiped my face with the sleeve of my coat. "I came back."

Three kids passed above us on the bridge, shouting and running.

"I'm a troll," whispered the troll, in a small, scared voice. "Fol rol de ol rol."

He was trembling.

I held out my hand, and took his huge, clawed paw in mine. I smiled at him. "It's okay," I told him. "Honestly. It's okay."

The troll nodded.

He pushed me to the ground, onto the leaves and the wrappers and the condom, and lowered himself on top of me. Then he raised his head, and opened his mouth, and ate my life with his strong sharp teeth.

§ § §

When he was finished, the troll stood up and brushed himself down. He put his hand into the pocket of his coat, and pulled out a bubbly, burnt lump of clinker rock.

He held it out to me.

"This is yours," said the troll.

I looked at him: wearing my life comfortably, easily, as if he'd been wearing it for years. I took the clinker from his hand, and sniffed it. I could smell the train from which it had fallen, so long ago. I gripped it tightly in my hairy hand.

"Thank you," I said.

"Good luck," said the troll.

"Yeah. Well. You too."

The troll grinned with my face.

It turned its back on me and began to walk back the way I had come, toward the village, back to the empty house I had left that morning; and it whistled as it walked.

I've been here ever since. Hiding. Waiting. Part of the bridge.

I watch from the shadows as the people pass: walking their dogs, or talking, or doing the things that people do. Sometimes people pause beneath my bridge, to stand, or piss, or make love. And I watch them, but say nothing; and they never see me.

Fol rol de ol rol.

I'm just going to stay here, in the darkness under the arch. I can hear you all out there, trip-trapping, trip-trapping over my bridge.

Oh yes, I can hear you.

But I'm not coming out.

VAMPIRE SESTINA

I wait here at the boundaries of dream,
all shadow-wrapped. The dark air tastes of night,
so cold and crisp, and I wait for my love.
The moon has bleached the colour from her stone.
She'll come, and then we'll stalk this pretty world
alive to darkness and the tang of blood.

It is a lonely game, the quest for blood,
but still, a body's got the right to dream
and I'd not give it up for all the world.
The moon has leeched the darkness from the night.
I stand in shadows, staring at her stone:
Undead, my lover... O, undead my love?

I dreamt you while I slept today and love
meant more to me than life — meant more than blood.
The sunlight sought me, deep beneath my stone,
more dead than any corpse but still a-dream
until I woke as vapour into night
and sunset forced me out into the world.

For many centuries I've walked the world
dispensing something that resembled love—
a stolen kiss, then back into the night
contented by the life and by the blood.
And come the morning I was just a dream,
cold body chilling underneath a stone.

VAMPIRE SESTINA

I said I would not hurt you. Am I stone
to leave you prey to time and to the world?
I offered you a truth beyond your dreams
while all *you* had to offer was your love.
I told you not to worry, and that blood
tastes sweeter on the wing and late at night.

Sometimes my lovers rise to walk the night...
Sometimes they lie, cold corpse beneath a stone,
and never know the joys of bed and blood,
of walking through the shadows of the world;
instead they rot to maggots. O my love
they whispered you had risen, in my dream.

I've waited by your stone for half the night
but you won't leave your dream to hunt for blood.
Goodnight, my love. I offered you the world.

WEBS

IN THE WEB-COVERED HALLS OF THE KING OF THE SPIDERS, Lupita spent a most memorable year. She had servants in attendance upon her, and a jerkin covered in chryolanths, a present from the King. Lupita was a guest of one of the Dark Lords, although nobody seemed to know which one; it was the subject of much court speculation:

"Today, milor' Lupita abased herself perhaps a trifle too low before Lord Caryatid."

"Ah, but yesterday she was seen publicly to ignore Lord Tistatte, and on one of the dark days: surely there is a sign of favour?"

"Or of other protection. Perhaps she is in lien to one of the Lords of shifting position..."

And all would be silent, and watch Lupita as she walked across the hall, strands of webbing adhering to her cape and drifting behind her like fronds of plants from the Slow Zone: old man's folly, perhaps, or tiger-whiskers, a plant spoken of in the classics as possessing certain unusual properties, although no one today knew nor cared what they were.

It was the uncertainty about Lupita's status that had kept her safe from court intrigues; for, after all, no one would dare to risk their status on a cheap guess. Blood was the Dark Lords' tithe from those who worshipped them, and few were overly eager to hasten the communion by involvement in the complicated and shifting game the Lords played. Instead they mirrored it, or thought they did, aped what they presumed they saw, with their petty little cliques, and their treacherous little factions.

Although the webs did much to mute sound in the endless corridors of the Palace of Spiders, there was always a soft susurrus, a sly whispering as alliances were formed, the hiss of betrayals discovered and bought, the kiss of character assassination (and possibly of assassination of another kind, for sometimes bodies could be seen lolling high in the webs of the halls, wrapped around in pale silken strands like empty insects in some old larder, although no one ever climbed the webbing to find out who it was that had been left there. The bodies were always gone in a week, or two at most).

In her time in the palace Lupita formed a number of oblique liaisons, but took no sexual partners, something which somehow was no surprise to anybody.

There was much that Lupita did to surprise, however.

She once went out hunting, and brought back a mammal, alive.

The King, before whom it was unveiled, said nothing, but signalled with a staff to the Chamberlain, who enquired:

"It is?"

"A cat, my Lord Chamberlain."

"And does it make good eating?"

(There was a ripple of appreciation at that: the Chamberlain had punned most elegantly, such that her words had also meant, *And is it given to men to eat their Gods?* and also, *Unravel this and we shall rejoice.*)

"No, my Lord Chamberlain, I do not believe that it does."

The animal stayed with her after that for many weeks. Then one morning, when mist hung low on the banqueting chamber and formed beads of moisture on the crouching iron bodies of the Dark Lords, the body of the cat was to be seen hanging some forty feet above the ground, in the webs, not far from Lupita's chambers.

A small crowd gathered.

Lupita rose at her usual hour. She came out of her chambers, but when she saw the crowd, and when she realized what they were looking at, she turned, with no expression, and went back in through the door from which she had come.

When she returned, about thirty minutes later, the crowd had swelled to almost a score of courtiers, and an equal number of others.

Lupita carried with her a basket containing a filled waterbladder, several small dry rolls, and some crystallised fruit. The black of her cloak had been replaced by a rich crimson, and she had placed a knife in her belt.

She took a crossbow from one of her servants, and aimed it at the mammal's wrapped body. The bolt made no noise when it struck home, trailing a thin thread behind it.

Lupita tied the thread around her thumb, then sat, cross-legged, on the floor of the corridor, and waited.

The crowd stared at her, enraptured, waiting with amazement for her next trick. It was all so new, so daring. Someone at the back began to applaud, swallowing gulps of air and belching loudly, but the noise was quickly shushed.

By the time the stone was struck for evening meal, the last onlooker had given up, and wandered off. Lupita was still waiting, sitting in the shadows, pale eyes gazing up at the shrouded body.

When the last stone was struck for deep night a servant came by and replaced the food and water Lupita had consumed on her vigil.

On the third night it seemed to Lupita almost as if the servant were about to speak to her, but the servant did no such thing. So Lupita spoke to the servant.

"Do you know what I will find?"

The servant shrugged.

"Do you care?"

"It is," admitted the servant, "not something that will affect my lot one way or another."

Lupita nodded dismissal, and the servant backed away.

It is said that at that time Lupita slept, and dreamed a dream. But a dream is a private matter, and we shall not concern ourselves with it. Be that as it may, Lupita was either woken, or not woken but alerted, an hour after this, by a tugging on the thread about her thumb. Looking up she could just make out the cat-cadaver lurching up the web. She let out loops of thread from her thumb, like someone coaxing a nervous kite to fly, until she saw the shape vanish in the webbing, pulled inside by a dark and spindly limb.

It was then that Lupita hand-over-handed up the web (which would have caused apoplexy, and perhaps a chorus of eructation, had an audience been there to observe), trying, and not altogether failing, to move at random, as if she were merely a rip in the net, old bones and gnawed skulls slipping and shifting from the turbulence in the web caused by the recent passage of the cat.

She waited near the spot where the mammal's body had vanished, until the thread was tight around her thumb (which she could feel was losing feeling), then she let out the last couple of loops, and pushed into the web. Strands of the stuff stuck to her eyelashes, her face, her hair. She screwed her eyes together tightly, then pulled her cloak in front of her face, and moved forward into the space.

She had expected a tunnel.

Instead she found herself disoriented, moving through something that felt like a waterfall, but which was composed of light and something else, not matter. It seemed like something was brushing her lightly from the soles of her feet to her head. It tickled, but it was a tickling inside, not outside, not on her skin.

Her eyes were still tight shut, but colours formed inside them, seeping like river mists of blue, of green, of peach and viridian, then exploding like fire inside her head.

She said nothing, and was still. When her inner world had calmed down she lowered her cloak, and opened her eyes. The world had turned silver: lights shone silver from mirrored panels, illuminated silver switches and buttons, cast silver reflections on silver surfaces and spilled to the silver floor around dark grey shadows.

In a corner, next to a vast metal ship, its silver sails fluttering in a non-existent breeze, sat two huge spiders, white spots on splotchy brown abdomens; angular knobby-jointed legs waving gently in the air; emerald eyes gleaming with hunger and greed.

They had divided the cat between them, and were eating it in a most unpleasant fashion.

Lupita pulled her knife from her belt, and threw it at the largest of the spiders, hitting it in the abdomen. White stuff began to ooze from the cut, dripping onto the metal floor. The creature ate on, not noticing the wound, not even when the pale substance (in appearance, Lupita observed, somewhere between pus and jelly) oozed as far as the cat, and the spider continued its meal with itself as sauce and condiment.

ANGELS AND VISITATIONS

Since her knife attack had done no apparent good, Lupita slowly began to circle the spiders, walking as quietly as was possible. She circled them once, twice, three times, then she ran, hard, as fast as she could toward a far wall.

She turned around, and winced. The thread had performed its function, but while one of the spiders — the one with the wounded belly — had been neatly sliced in two, yellow organs swimming in mucus now slipping and spilling onto the floor, the other had been less fortunate. The thread had slid down, so that, instead of encircling the body, it had merely noosed the legs. The final tug had pulled seven of the eight legs off, and they lay stiff and ghastly on the ground, stacked up like dreadful brushwood against the spider's shivering body. The last leg twitched and spasmed, spinning the spider around on the silver floor.

Lupita went close enough to it to retrieve her knife, then, keeping well clear of the mouth, which was opening and closing in impotent and silent fury, she slit the creature's belly wide open, with a cry,

"*Haih!*" and jumped back, pulling up her cloak as she did so to avoid the tumbling organs splashing it.

She tried to untie the thread from her thumb, but it had been too tightly wound for too long, and her thumb was blue and cold. The thread had been pulled too tight to untie and was too tough to cut, although she produced a respectable amount of blood in trying.

In the end she had to cut the thumb off. She cauterised it in spider-spit, which took away the pain and stopped the bleeding, although it made her feel strangely distant, as if she was not participating in her life, but was merely an interested spectator, watching her own actions from over her shoulder. This feeling, which was new to her, was to recur several times in later life.

She wiped the knife on her leg, returned it to her belt, and climbed out the way she had come.

The next day it was observed that neither the King nor the Lord Chamberlain were to be found in the palace environs; however this realization was rapidly overshadowed by the discovery that a certain antique Dark Lord had gone into fugue, and was apparently blown out.

Angels and Visitations

It was widely assumed that Lupita had cut off her thumb in order to appear mysterious, and the court, unable to cope with further mysteries, agreed to find this in faintly bad taste.

Worse was to follow:

That evening Lupita left the palace. Before she went, as she passed through the hall of the Dark Lords, she was seen to stroke the casing of the Lord-in-fugue.

The court gathered in an observation tower to watch her leave; they stared after her until she had crossed the borderline and was lost in the mists; but the sky remained curiously free from lightning, there were no awful screams or terrible cries, and the earth did not part and swallow her up.

They went back to their halls feeling slightly let down. Later they polished the Dark Lords: Iliaster and Baraquely, Zibanitu-tula, Ettanin, Bodstieriyan, and the rest.

It was then that one of the lesser courtiers was foolish enough to be heard praying that Lupita be punished for her lack of respect. Prayers of any kind were anathema to the Dark Lords, and he was turned to twisted stone where he stood.

The people waited for their king and his chamberlain to return to them.

The webs collapsed and rotted in the halls near to where Lupita (now just an enigmatic memory) had had her chambers. But other webs were being spun; they were all over the palace, if you knew where to look for them.

Six to Six

"Oh, don't do nightspots," says My Editor, "someone's already done them. Can you do somewhere else?"

I crumple up a carefully planned evening that takes in every London nightspot I've ever been to and a few I haven't. Fine. I'll just play it as it comes, then. Maybe hang around the West End streets. I tell her this.

She seems vaguely concerned. "Be careful," she warns. Warmed and heartened, pondering imaginary obituary notices, and adventures ahead, I stumble out into the late afternoon.

Six till six.

6:00   I'm seeing my bank manager. We're standing out in the hall, discussing the use of the word *fucking* in contemporary magazine articles. I tell him I can use *fucking* in *Time Out* whenever I want, at which point someone with a suit glides out of an office and stares at us. The tinkling laughter of his singular secretary, Maggie, follows me as I flee.

I try to get a cab at Baker Street, but the yellow 'TAXI' light, holy grail of London emergencies, proves usually elusive. I tube to Tottenham Court Road, where a queue of taxis lurk, yellow lights blazing.

Head down to the basement of My Publishers, make some phone calls, stumble over the road to the Café München in the shadow of Centre Point, where I drink with Temporary *Crisis* Editor James Robinson, awaiting the arrival of My Publisher.

Angels and Visitations

My Publisher is late but I bump into huge rock star Fish (late of Marillion); we haven't seen each other for years, and catch up on recent events, interrupted only by a shady-looking fellow who's setting up 'the biggest charity in England' and wants Fish to lend support, and a prat who asks Fish to write out the lyrics to 'Kayleigh' on a napkin so he can win a £50 bet. Fish says he can't remember them and sends the guy away with an autograph. Still, somebody made £50 off of it.

My Publisher turns up, and we head off to grab something to eat (La Reach in Old Compton Street, great couscous), promising to meet Fish later in the new, moved Marquee. He'll put our names on the door.

11:15   We turn up at the Marquee to be met by "Sorry mate — we closed at 11:00". When I was a teenager the Marquee (possibly the cheapest sauna in the metropolis) scarcely opened before eleven. Dreams of a peculiar rock-n'-rolloid night vanish. I still don't know what I'm going to be doing this evening.

My Publisher is heading down to Wimbledon to try and fix an antique laserdisc player he'd sold to an old friend. I go with him.

1:00   Laserdisc player still doesn't work, which means my publisher is unable to view *Miami Spice* ("Those Miami Spice girls sure have a nose for torrid trouble...a porno pool party...our passionate policewomen are ready for the big bust..." Fnur fnur).

1:30   Driving back into town through empty Wimbledon we get pulled over by a police car — they've noticed the antique laserdisc player in the boot, and have leapt to the not unreasonable conclusion that My Publisher is in fact a burglar. Nervously he hides *Miami Spice* under the seat, gets out of the car, hands the cop his mobile phone and tells him to phone people to prove his identity; the cop stares at it wistfully. "They won't even give us one of those," he sighs. He asks My Publisher about his (Barrow in Furness) accent and announces that he comes from Bridlington himself. Waves us on our way. My plans of an exciting night crusading against police brutality — or better yet, journalistically, spent in the cells — founder and crash.

1:45   Victoria Station. *Something* must be happening at Victoria...nope. A sterile expanse, full of fluorescent ads for things you can't buy at this time of night. (Prawn Waldorf sandwiches?) My Publisher explains that London pigeons have lost their toes through decades of inbreeding and pollution. Tell him this sounds unlikely.

2:10   Pass the Hard Rock Café. Nobody's queuing.

2:45   Soho. We walk past a street of empty wine bars and book shops, and My Publisher tells me it used to be brothels once, a long time ago; then, *Miami Spice* and a functioning laserdisc player ahead of him, he tears off into the night.

I decide that I'm just going to wander aimlessly, resolve not to disappear into any seedy drinking clubs, even if I can find any (like Little Magic Shops, they have a tendency to vanish the next time you want them, replaced by brick walls or closed doors).

Under the tacky neon glare of Brewer Street a young woman holds a polystyrene head with a red wig on it. The Vintage Magazine Shop has the OZ "schoolkids" issue in the window.

3:31   At a tacky all-night food place — *Mr Pumpernincks* — on the corner of Piccadilly, I run into Ella. She's blonde, with smudged pink lipstick and red pumps, dayglo acidhouse wristbands. Looks fifteen, assures me she's really nearly nineteen and tells me not to eat the popcorn because it "tastes like ear-wax".

Turns out she's a nightclub hostess. I assume this is my first encounter tonight with the seamy side of London nightlife. She shakes her head. Her job, she explains, is to sell as much champagne as possible on commission, pour her glass on the floor when the customer "goes to the loo", spill as much as she can. It's all a con, she sighs: £12 for a salmon sandwich, £12 for a packet of 40 cigarettes, no-one spends less than £100 a night, and last week she was offered £5000 by five Swedish men to sleep with them.

She said no. She doesn't think she's hard enough for this business. Ella comes down to Mr Pumpernincks to drink the rotten coffee and sober up every night. She came up from Bath to the big city a month or so back; her

51

ambition in life is to steal a Porsche 911 Turbo, and possibly even to get a driving license.

4:30 I'm in Brewer Street again. Six pigeons on the road in front of me; one of them doesn't have any toes. My Publisher was right.

In Wardour Street a small heap of Goths huddle together, walking warily. I can't figure out why: there's no-one around to menace them, but maybe they don't know that.

It's sort of boring; there's simply no-one about. I start fantasising a mugging to break up the monotony of empty chill streets; I could probably claim it back on expenses.

Ella's gone the next time I pass Piccadilly.

In one of the back streets behind Shaftesbury Avenue, I walk past some accordion doors with something written on them. Walking toward them it reads OPRIG. Parallel it says NO PARKING. Looking back over my shoulder it reads N AKN. I wonder briefly if somebody is trying to tell me something, then conclude I'm getting tired, or transcendently bored.

On the Charing Cross Road a little old Chinese lady teeter-totters on the pavement, gesturing at taxis that ignore her. She looks lost. Leicester Square is utterly deserted.

It's nearly 5:00AM. I stop a couple of cops I've seen across roads all evening. Ask them about the West End — is there *anything* happening late at night? They say no, say the area's still cruising on a reputation it hasn't deserved for over a decade. They sigh, wistfully. "You may get the odd rent boy hanging round Piccadilly, but that's all they do: hang around."

They'd seen three people in their last sweep through every dangerous dead-end alley and mysterious Soho street. They're almost as bored as I am; I'm probably the most interesting thing that's happened to them all night. If I had a mobile phone I'd let them play with it. 5:30, they tell me, things hot up; the cleaners begin to come round.

5:20 I pass a McDonald's. Already the McPeople who work there are in, McScrubbing the McCounters and unloading McMillions of McBuns from the McTruck.

Angels and Visitations

5:40   Ponder the touching concern in My Editor's voice when I told her I'd wander the streets, her obvious worry that terrible things were going to happen to me. I should have been so lucky.

6:02   I'm in the taxi going home. I tell the driver about my abortive evening. "Fing is," he explains, "Everybody relates to Wardour Street, Brewer Street, Greek Street as where the action is. They fink people hang round the 'Dilly still, addicts waiting for their scrips. Fuck me man, you're going back twenty years. Notting Hill, that's where it's all at these days. The action's always there. It just moves. And the West End's been cleaned up so hard it's dead."

Conclusion: (Statistical breakdown)

murders seen	0
car chases involved in	0
adventures had	0
foreign spies encountered	0
ladies of the night ditto	1/2 (Ella)
rock stars encountered (in Café München)	1
encounters with police	2

A PROLOGUE

AN INTRODUCTION TO MARY GENTLE'S *SCHOLARS & SOLDIERS*

Scene: A fairground. Persons of anachronistic but stylish demeanour and dress walk back and forth, juggling fire, elegant cats, faster-than-light drives and extremely sharp blades. Dancing bears tread lumbering pavanes, and hawkers sell candied plums and overspiced cuts of roast lizard.

In the centre of the fair is a brightly coloured tent, and in front of that, a raised platform. From the tent steps a Prologue, in black motley, carrying a scroll. He unrolls it, and commences to read:

"The author bade me come to introduce her tales —" He pauses. Pulls out a quill pen, scritches out a word or two, begins again. "Now, Mistress Gentle bade me come to introduce her tales (which follow this) to all of you..."

A soldier in the crowd, her fancy-boy on one arm, waves at him, and shouts, "This Mistress Gentle. She's an author, then?"

The Prologue nods.

"I always thought that authors were fabulous beasts," says the soldier, with the air of someone misquoting deliberately (proving herself, perhaps, something of a scholar).

"Some of us are, some of us aren't," says the Prologue, preening slightly.

The soldier frowns, "So. This author of yours, Mistress, um..."

"Gentle."

"Right. Mistress Gentle. What kind of an author is she?"

The Prologue lays down his scroll regretfully, and sighs. "The better sort. Like all the very best authors she dresses in black, reads comics — *Love and Rockets*, for preference — devoured an unhealthy amount of science fiction (and everything else) as a kid, knows her way around Croydon..."

"Is that important?" asks the soldier.

"Essential." The Prologue takes up his scroll, and is about to begin once more, when the soldier asks:

"But what kind of an author is she?"

The Prologue hesitates.

Another member of the audience (fat, huge as Chesterton or Aquinas, with globs of lizard-fat still adhering to his chin) chips in: "The way I see it, she's part of the late-twentieth-century cultural fusion. The melting pot (in its true meaning as crucible) that brings forth, occasionally, gold from dross. In the stories that follow we can see her gradually assimilating her influences: from glittery SF to Restoration Drama, from Low Tragedy to High Comedy, from punk comic books to Hermetic philosophy, from courtly fantasy to uncouth horror (and, given her cultural parameters, vice versa), finally producing something distinctly, uniquely her own."

"Yeah. What he said," agrees the Prologue, picking up his scroll, and clearing his throat. "Ahem! Mistress Gentle bade me come this day to introduce her stories to you all. For here are knights and gallants, and alarums, and here are fantasies and flights historical, futurities (the fair, the dark, the lost), and —"

"Look, that's quite enough of that," interrupts the soldier, her hand on her sword hilt. "What kind of an author is she?"

The Prologue puts his scroll inside his battered black leather jacket; asks testily, "What exactly are you asking?"

"Just what I said."

He sighs. "Okay. Her hair is currently reddish..." An idea strikes him. He reaches back into his jacket pocket, pulls out a first quarto of *Antony and Cleopatra*, leafs through it, cracked, yellowed paper falling like confetti, and reads:

> *Lepidus: What manner of thing is your crocodile?*
> *Antony: It is shaped, sir, just like itself, and it is as broad as it hath*
> *   breadth; it is just so high as it is, and moves with its own*
> *   organs; it lives by that which nourisheth it; and the ele-*
> *   ments once out of it, it transmigrates.*
> *Lepidus: What colour is it of?*

Antony: Of its own colour too.
Lepidus: 'Tis a strange serpent.
Antony: 'Tis so; and the tears of it are wet.

He puts the script away, adjusts his shades. "There."

The soldier sighs, tiring of this discussion, eager to be off. "So Mistress Gentle...?"

"Is a strange serpent, yes."

She turns on her heel, pauses, turns her head, and says, "There's still one question you haven't answered."

"And that is?"

"What kind of an author is she?"

The Prologue grins. "Prologues never tell you. For that you gotta read the stories."

The soldier nods, curtly, and leaves.

The Prologue walks back into his tent, and he too is gone.

Outside the hawkers offer passers-by sweetmeats and roasted lizards, the tumblers continue to tumble, the small animals, coloured balls, asteroids and dice follow each other through the air, the courtesans (of all sexes) continue to ply their trade, and the bears still dance; the soldiers and the scholars walk together and in the gathering dusk it is increasingly difficult to tell them apart...

FOREIGN PARTS

The VENEREAL DISEASE is a disease contracted as a consequence of impure connexion. The fearful constitutional consequences which may result from this affection, — consequences, the fear of which may haunt the mind for years, which may taint the whole springs of health, and be transmitted to circulate in the young blood of innocent offspring, — are indeed terrible considerations, too terrible not to render the disease one of those which must unhesitatingly be placed under medical care.

Spencer Thomas, M.D., L.R.C.S. (Edin.)
A Dictionary of Domestic Medicine and Household Surgery: 1882.

SIMON POWERS DIDN'T LIKE SEX. Not really.

He disliked having someone else in the same bed as himself; he suspected that he came too soon; he always felt uncomfortably that his performance was in some way being graded, like a driving test, or a practical examination.

He had got laid in college a few times, and once, three years ago, after the office New Year's party. But that had been that, and as far as Simon was concerned he was well out of it.

It occurred to him once, during a slack time at the office, that he would have liked to have lived in the days of Queen Victoria, where well brought up women were no more than resentful sex-dolls in the bedroom: they'd unlace their stays, loosen their petticoats (revealing pinkish-white flesh), then lie back and suffer the indignities of the carnal act — an indignity it would never even occur to them that they were meant to enjoy.

He filed it away for later, another masturbatory fantasy.

Simon masturbated a great deal. Every night — sometimes more than that, if he was unable to sleep. He could take as long, or as short, a time to climax as he wished. And in his mind, he had had them all. Film and television stars; women from the office; schoolgirls; the naked models who pouted from the crumpled pages of *Fiesta*; faceless slaves in chains; tanned boys with bodies like Greek gods...

Night after night they paraded in front of him.

It was safer that way.

In his mind.

And afterward he'd fall asleep, comfortable and safe in a world he controlled, and he'd sleep without dreaming. Or at least, he never remembered his dreams in the morning.

The morning it started he was woken by the radio ("...two hundred killed and many others believed to be injured; and now over to Jack for the weather and traffic news..."), dragged himself out of bed, and stumbled, bladder aching, into the bathroom.

He pulled up the toilet seat, and urinated. It felt like he was pissing needles.

He needed to urinate again after breakfast — less painfully, since the flow was not as heavy — and three more times before lunch.

Each time it hurt.

He told himself that it couldn't be a venereal disease. That was something that other people got, and something (he thought of his last sexual encounter, three years in the past) that you got from other people. You couldn't really catch it from toilet seats, could you? Wasn't that just a joke?

Simon Powers was twenty-six, and he worked in a large London bank, in the securities division. He had few friends at work. His only real friend, Nick Lawrence, a lonely Canadian, had recently transferred to another branch, and Simon sat by himself in the staff canteen, staring out at the Docklands Lego landscape, picking at a limp green salad.

Someone tapped him on the shoulder.

"Simon, I heard a good one today. Wanna hear?" Jim Jones was the office clown, a dark-haired, intense young man, who claimed he had a special pocket on his boxer shorts, for condoms.

"Um. Sure."

"Here you go. What's the collective noun for people who work in banks?"

"The what?"

"Collective noun. You know, like a flock of sheep, a pride of lions. Give up?"

Simon nodded.

"A Wunch of Bankers."

Simon must have looked puzzled, because Jim sighed and said, "Wunch of Bankers. *Bunch* of *Wankers*. God, you're slow...." Then, spotting a group of young women at a far table, Jim straightened his tie, and carried his tray over to them.

He could hear Jim telling his joke to the women, this time with added hand movements.

They all got it immediately.

Simon left his salad on the table, and went back to work.

That night he sat in his chair, in his bedsitter flat, with the television turned off, and he tried to remember what he knew about venereal diseases.

There was syphilis, that pocked your face and drove the Kings of England mad; gonorrhea — the clap — a green oozing, and more madness; crabs, little pubic lice, which nested and itched (he inspected his pubic hairs through a magnifying glass, but nothing moved); AIDS, the eighties plague, a plea for clean needles and safer sexual habits (but what could be safer than a clean wank for one into a fresh handful of white tissues?); herpes, which had something to do with cold sores (he checked his lips in the mirror, they looked fine). That was all he knew.

And he went to bed, and fretted himself to sleep, without daring to masturbate.

That night he dreamed of tiny women with blank faces, walking in endless rows between gargantuan office blocks, like an army of soldier ants.

Simon did nothing about the pain for another two days. He hoped it would go away, or get better on its own. It didn't. It got worse. The pain continued for up to an hour after urination; his penis felt raw and bruised inside.

And on the third day, he phoned his doctor's surgery to make an appointment. He had dreaded having to tell the woman who answered the phone what the problem was, and so he was relieved, and perhaps just a little disappointed, when she didn't ask, but simply made an appointment for the following day.

He told his senior at the bank that he had a sore throat, and would need to see the doctor about it. He could feel his cheeks burn as he told her, but she did not remark on this, merely told him that that would be fine.

When he left her office he found that he was shaking.

It was a grey, wet day when he arrived at the doctor's surgery. There was no queue, and he went straight in to the doctor. Not his regular doctor, Simon was comforted to see. This was a young Pakistani, of about Simon's age, who interrupted Simon's stammered recitation of symptoms to ask:

"Urinating more than usual, are we?"

Simon nodded.

"Any discharge?"

Simon shook his head.

"Right ho. I'd like you to take down your trousers, if you don't mind."

Simon took them down. The doctor peered at his penis. "You do have a discharge, you know," he said.

Simon did himself up again.

"Now, Mr Powers, tell me, do you think it possible that you might have picked up from someone, a, uh, venereal disease?"

Simon shook his head vigorously. "I haven't had sex with anyone —" he had almost said, 'anyone else' "— in almost three years."

"No?" The doctor obviously didn't believe him. He smelled of exotic spices, and had the whitest teeth Simon had ever seen. "Well, you have either contracted gonorrhea or NSU. Probably NSU: Non Specific Urethritis. Which is less famous and less painful than gonorrhea, but it can be a bit of an old bastard to treat. You can get rid of gonorrhea with one big dose of antibiotics. Kills the bugger off..." He clapped his hands, twice. Loudly. "Just like that."

"You don't know, then?"

"Which one it is? Good Lord, no. I'm not even going to try to find out. I'm sending you to a special clinic, which takes care of all of that kind of thing. I'll give you a note to take with you." He pulled a pad of headed notepaper from a drawer. "What is your profession, Mr Powers?"

"I work in a bank."

"A teller?"

"No." He shook his head. "I'm in securities. I clerk for two assistant managers." A thought occurred to him. "They don't have to know about this, do they?"

The doctor looked shocked. "Good gracious, no."

He wrote a note, in a careful, round handwriting, stating that Simon Powers, age 26, had something that was probably NSU. He had a discharge. Said he had had no sex for three years. In discomfort. Please could they let him know the results of the tests. He signed it with a squiggle. Then he handed Simon a card, with the address and phone number of the special clinic on it. "Here you are. This is where you go. Not to worry — happens to lots of people. See all the cards I have here? Not to worry — you'll soon be right as rain. Phone them when you get home and make an appointment."

Simon took the card, and stood up to go.

"Don't worry," said the doctor. "It won't prove difficult to treat."

Simon nodded, and tried to smile.

He opened the door, to go out.

"And at any rate it's nothing really nasty, like syphilis," said the doctor.

The two elderly women sitting outside in the hallway waiting area looked up delightedly at this fortuitous overheard, and stared hungrily at Simon as he walked away.

He wished he were dead.

On the pavement outside, waiting for the bus home, Simon thought: *I've got a venereal disease. I've got a venereal disease. I've got a venereal disease.* Over and over, like a mantra.

He should toll a bell as he walked.

On the bus he tried not to get too close to his fellow passengers. He was certain they knew (couldn't they read the plague-marks on his face?); and at the same time he was ashamed he was forced to keep it a secret from them.

He got back to the flat and went straight into the bathroom, expecting to see a decayed horror-movie face, a rotting skull fuzzy with blue mould, staring back at him from the mirror. Instead he saw a pink-cheeked bank clerk in his mid-twenties, fair-haired, perfect-skinned.

He fumbled out his penis and scrutinised it with care. It was neither a gangrenous green nor a leprous white, but looked perfectly normal, except for the slightly swollen tip and the clear discharge that lubricated the hole. He realised that his white underpants had been stained across the crotch by the leak.

Simon felt angry with himself, and angrier with God for having given him a (say it) (*dose of the clap*) obviously meant for someone else.

He masturbated that night, for the first time in four days.

He fantasised a schoolgirl, in blue cotton panties, who changed into a policewoman, then two policewomen, then three.

It didn't hurt at all, until he climaxed; then he felt as if someone were pushing a switchblade through the inside of his cock. As if he were ejaculating a pin-cushion.

He began to cry then, in the darkness, but whether from the pain, or from some other reason, less easy to identify, even Simon was unsure.

That was the last time he masturbated.

§ § §

The clinic was located in a dour Victorian hospital in central London. A young man in a white coat looked at Simon's card, and took his doctor's note, and told him to take a seat.

Simon sat down on an orange plastic chair covered with brown cigarette burns.

He stared at the floor for a few minutes. Then, having exhausted that form of entertainment, he stared at the walls, and finally, having no other option, at the other people.

They were all male, thank god — women were on the next floor up — and there were more than a dozen of them:

The most comfortable were the macho building-site types, here for their seventeenth or seventieth time, looking rather pleased with themselves, as if whatever they had caught were proof of their virility. There were a few city gents, in ties and suits. One of them looked relaxed; he carried a mobile tele-phone. Another, hiding behind a *Daily Telegraph*, was blushing, embarrassed to be there; there were little men with wispy moustaches and tatty raincoats — newspaper sellers, perhaps, or retired teachers; a rotund oriental gentle-man, who chain-smoked filterless cigarettes, lighting each cigarette from the butt of the one before, so the flame never went out, but was transmitted from one dying cigarette to the next. In one corner sat a scared gay couple. Neither of them looked more than eighteen. This was obviously their first appoint-ment as well, the way they kept glancing around. They were holding hands, white-knuckled and discreetly. They were terrified.

Simon felt comforted. He felt less alone.

"Mister Powers, please," said the man at the desk. Simon stood up, con-scious that all eyes were upon him, that he'd been identified and named in front of all these people. A cheerful, red-haired doctor in a white coat was waiting.

"Follow me," he said.

They walked down some corridors, through a door (on which *DR. J. BENHAM* was written in felt pen on a white sheet of paper sellotaped to the frosted glass), into a doctor's office.

"I'm Doctor Benham," said the doctor. He didn't offer to shake hands. "You have a note from your doctor?"

"I gave it to the man at the desk."

"Oh." Dr Benham opened a file on the desk in front of him. There was a computer-printout label on the side. It said:

REG'D 2 JLY 90. MALE. 90/00666.L

POWERS, SIMON, MR.

BORN 12 OCT 63. SINGLE.

Benham read the note, looked at Simon's penis, and handed him a sheet of blue paper from the file. It had the same label, stuck to the top.

"Take a seat in the corridor," he told him. "A nurse will collect you."

Simon waited in the corridor.

"They're very fragile," said the sunburnt man sitting next to him, by accent a South African, or perhaps Zimbabwean. Colonial accent, at any rate.

"I'm sorry?"

"Very fragile. Venereal diseases. Think about it. You can catch a cold or flu simply by being in the same room as someone who's got it. Venereal diseases need warmth and moisture, and intimate contact."

Not mine, thought Simon, but he didn't say anything.

"You know what I'm dreading?" said the South African.

Simon shook his head.

"Telling my wife," said the man, and he fell silent.

A nurse came and took Simon away. She was young, and pretty, and he followed her into a cubicle. She took the blue slip of paper from him.

"Take off your jacket and roll up your right sleeve."

"My jacket?"

She sighed. "For the blood test."

"Oh."

The blood test was almost pleasant, compared to what came next.

"Take down your trousers," she told him. She had a marked Australian accent. His penis had shrunk, tightly pulled in on itself; it looked grey and wrinkled. He found himself wanting to tell her that it was normally much larger, but then she picked up a metal instrument with a wire loop at the end, and he wished it were even smaller. "Squeeze your penis at the base, and push forward a few times." He did so. She stuck the loop into the head of his penis and twisted it around inside. He winced at the pain. She smeared the discharge onto a glass slide. Then she pointed to a glass jar on a shelf. "Can you urinate into that for me, please?"

"What, from here?"

She pursed her lips. Simon suspected that she must have heard that joke thirty times a day since she had been working there.

She went out of the cubicle and left him alone to pee.

Simon found it difficult to pee at the best of times, often having to wait around in toilets until all the people had gone. He envied men who could casually walk into toilets, unzip, and carry on cheerful conversations with their neighbours in the adjoining urinal, all the while showering the white porcelain with yellow urine. Often he couldn't do it at all.

65

He couldn't do it now.

The nurse came in again. "No luck? Not to worry. Take a seat back in the waiting room, and the doctor will call you in a minute."

"Well," said Dr Benham. "You have NSU. Non Specific Urethritis."

Simon nodded, and then he said, "What does that mean?"

"It means you don't have gonorrhea, Mr Powers."

"But I haven't had sex with, with anyone, for..."

"Oh, that's nothing to worry about. It can be a quite spontaneous disease — you need not, um, indulge, to pick it up." Benham reached into a desk drawer and pulled out a bottle of pills. "Take one of these four times a day, before meals. Stay off alcohol, no sex, and don't drink milk for a couple of hours after taking one. Got it?"

Simon grinned nervously.

"I'll see you next week. Make an appointment downstairs."

Downstairs they gave him a red card with his name on and the time of his appointment. It also had a number on: 90/00666.L.

Walking home in the rain, Simon paused outside a travel agents'. The poster in the window showed a beach in the sun, and three bronzed women in bikinis, sipping long drinks.

Simon had never been abroad.

Foreign places made him nervous.

As the week went on the pain went away; and four days later Simon found himself able to urinate without flinching.

Something else was happening, however.

It began as a tiny seed, which took root in his mind, and grew. He told Dr Benham about it, on his next appointment.

Benham was puzzled.

"You're saying that you don't feel your penis is your own anymore, then, Mr Powers?"

"That's right, Doctor."

"I'm afraid I don't quite follow you. Is there some kind of loss of sensation?"

Simon could feel his penis inside his trousers, felt the sensation of cloth against flesh. In the darkness it began to stir.

"Not at all. I can feel everything like I always could. It's just it feels... well, different, I suppose. Like it isn't really part of me any more. Like it..." He paused. "...Like it belongs to someone else."

Dr Benham shook his head. "To answer your question, Mr Powers, that isn't a symptom of NSU — although it's a perfectly valid psychological reaction for someone who has contracted it. A, uh, feeling of disgust with yourself, perhaps, which you've externalised as a rejection of your genitalia."

That sounds about right, thought Dr Benham. He hoped he had got the jargon correct. He had never paid much attention to his psychology lectures or textbooks, which might explain, or so his wife maintained, why he was currently serving out a stint in a London VD clinic.

Powers looked a little soothed.

"I was just a bit worried, Doctor, that's all." He chewed his lower lip. "Um, what exactly *is* NSU?"

Benham smiled, reassuringly. "Could be any one of a number of things. NSU is just our way of saying we don't know exactly what it is. 'Non Specific', you see. It's an infection, and it responds to antibiotics. Which reminds me..." He opened a desk drawer, and took out a new week's supply.

"Make an appointment downstairs for next week. No sex. No alcohol."

No sex? thought Simon. *Not bloody likely.*

But when he walked past the pretty Australian nurse, in the corridor, he felt his penis begin to stir again; begin to get warm, and to harden.

§   §   §

Benham saw Simon the following week. Tests showed he still had the disease.

Benham shrugged.

"It's not unusual for it to hang on for this long. You say you feel no discomfort?"

"No. None at all. And I haven't seen any discharge either."

Benham was tired, and a dull pain throbbed behind his left eye. He glanced down at the tests, in the folder. "You've still got it, I'm afraid."

ANGELS AND VISITATIONS

Simon Powers shifted in his seat. He had large, watery blue eyes, and a pale, unhappy face. "What about the other thing, Doctor?"

The doctor shook his head. "What other thing?"

"I *told* you," said Simon. "Last week. I *told* you. The feeling that my, um, my penis, wasn't, isn't *my* penis any more."

Of course, thought Benham. It's *that* patient. There was never any way he could remember the procession of names and faces and penises, with their awkwardness, and their braggadocio, and their sweaty nervous smells, and their sad little diseases.

"Mm. What about it?"

"It's spreading, Doctor. The whole lower half of my body feels like it's someone else's. My legs, and everything. I can feel them all right, and they go where I want them to go, but sometimes I get the feeling that if they wanted to go somewhere else — if they wanted to go walking off into the world — they could, and they'd take me with them.

"I wouldn't be able to do anything to stop it."

Benham shook his head. He hadn't really been listening. "We'll change your antibiotics. If the others haven't knocked this disease out by now, I'm sure these will. They'll probably get rid of this other feeling as well — it's probably just a side effect of the antibiotics."

The young man just stared at him.

Benham felt he should say something else. "Perhaps you should try to get out more," he said.

The young man stood up.

"Same time next week. No sex, no booze, no milk after the pills." The doctor recited his litany.

The young man walked away. Benham watched him carefully, but could see nothing strange about the way he walked.

§   §   §

On Saturday night, Dr Jeremy Benham and his wife, Celia, attended a dinner party, held by a professional colleague. Benham sat next to a foreign psychiatrist.

68

They began to talk over the hors d'oeuvres.

"The trouble with telling folks you're a psychiatrist," said the psychiatrist, who was American, and huge, and bullet-headed, and looked like a merchant marine, "is you get to watch them trying to act normal for the rest of the evening." He chuckled, low and dirty.

Benham chuckled too, and since he was sitting next to a psychiatrist, he spent the rest of the evening trying to act normally.

He drank too much wine with his dinner.

After the coffee, when he couldn't think of anything else to say, he told the psychiatrist (whose name was Marshall, although he told Benham to call him Mike) what he could recall of Simon Powers' delusions.

Mike laughed. "Sounds fun. Maybe a tiny bit spooky. But nothing to worry about. Probably just a hallucination caused by a reaction to the antibiotics. Sounds a little like Capgras's Syndrome. You heard about that over here?"

Benham nodded, then thought, then said, "No". He poured himself another glass of wine, ignoring his wife's pursed lips and almost imperceptibly shaken head.

"Well, Capgras's Syndrome," said Mike, "is this funky delusion. Whole piece on it in *The Journal of American Psychiatry*, about five years back. Basically, it's where a person believes that the important people in his or her life — family members, workmates, parents, loved ones, whatever — have been replaced by — get this! — exact doubles.

"Doesn't apply to everyone they know. Just selected people. Often just one person in their life. No accompanying delusions, either. Just that one thing. Acutely emotionally disturbed people, with paranoid tendencies."

The psychiatrist picked his nose with his thumbnail. "I ran into a case myself, couple two-three years back."

"Did you cure him?"

The psychiatrist gave Benham a sideways look, and grinned, showing all his teeth. "In psychiatry, Doctor — unlike, perhaps, the world of sexually transmitted disease clinics — there is no such thing as a cure. There is only adjustment."

Benham sipped the red wine. Later it occurred to him that he would never have said what he said next, if it wasn't for the wine. Not aloud, anyway. "I don't suppose..." he paused, remembering a film he had seen as a teenager (something about *bodysnatchers*?), "I don't suppose that anyone ever checked to see if those people had been removed and replaced by exact doubles...?"

Mike — Marshall — whatever — gave Benham a very funny look indeed, and turned around in his chair to talk to his neighbour on the other side.

Benham for his part carried on trying to act normally (whatever that was) and failed miserably. He got very drunk indeed, started muttering about 'fucking colonials', and had a blazing row with his wife after the party was over, none of which were particularly normal occurrences.

§   §   §

Benham's wife locked him out of their bedroom, after the argument.

He lay on the sofa downstairs, covered by a crumpled blanket, and masturbated into his underpants, his hot seed spurting across his stomach.

In the small hours he was woken by a cold sensation around his loins.

He wiped himself off with his dress shirt, and returned to sleep.

§   §   §

Simon was unable to masturbate.

He wanted to, but his hand wouldn't move. It lay beside him, healthy, fine; but it was as if he had forgotten how to make it respond. Which was silly, wasn't it?

Wasn't it?

He began to sweat. It dripped from his face and forehead onto the white cotton sheets, but the rest of his body was dry.

Cell by cell something was reaching up inside him. It brushed his face, tenderly, like the kiss of a lover; it was licking his throat, breathing on his cheek. Touching him.

He had to get out of the bed. He couldn't get out of the bed.

He tried to scream, but his mouth wouldn't open. His larynx refused to vibrate.

Simon could still see the ceiling, lit by the lights of passing cars. The ceiling blurred: his eyes were still his own, and tears were oozing out of them, hot down his face, soaking the pillow.

They don't know what I've got, he thought. *They said I had what everyone else gets. But I didn't catch that. I've caught something different.*

Or maybe, he thought, as his vision clouded over, and the darkness swallowed the last of Simon Powers, *it caught me.*

Soon after that Simon got up, and washed, and inspected himself carefully in front of the bathroom mirror. Then he smiled, as if he liked what he saw.

§   §   §

Benham smiled. "I'm pleased to tell you," he said, "that I can give you a clean bill of health."

Simon Powers stretched in his seat, lazily, and nodded. "I feel terrific," he said.

He did look well, Benham thought. Glowing with health. He seemed taller as well. A very attractive young man, decided the doctor. "So, uh, no more of those feelings?"

"Feelings?"

"Those feelings you were telling me about. That your body didn't belong to you any more."

Simon waved a hand, gently, fanning his face. The cold weather had broken, and London was stewing in a sudden heatwave; it didn't feel like England any more.

Simon seemed amused.

"All of this body belongs to me, Doctor. I'm certain of that."

Simon Powers (90/00666.L SINGLE. MALE.) grinned like the world belonged to him as well.

The doctor watched him as he walked out of the surgery. He looked stronger, now; less fragile.

The next patient on Jeremy Benham's appointment card was a twenty-two-year-old boy. Benham was going to have to tell him he was HIV positive. *I hate this job,* he thought. *I need a holiday.*

71

He walked down the corridor to call the boy in, and pushed past Simon Powers, talking animatedly to a pretty young Australian Nurse. "... it must be a lovely place," he was telling her. "I want to see it. I want to go every-where. I want to meet *everyone*." He was resting a hand on her arm, and she was making no move to free herself from it.

Dr Benham stopped beside them. He touched Simon on the shoulder. "Young man," he said. "Don't let me see you back here."

Simon Powers grinned. "You won't see me here again, Doctor," he said. "Not as such, anyway. I've packed in my job. I'm going around the world."

They shook hands. Powers' hand was warm and comfortable and dry.

Benham walked away, but could not avoid hearing Simon Powers, still talking to the nurse.

"It's going to be so great," he was saying to her. Benham wondered if he was talking about sex, or world travel, or possibly, in some way, both.

"I'm going to have such *fun*," said Simon. "I'm loving it already."

Cold Colours

I.

Woken at nine o'clock by the postman
Who turns out not to be the postman but an itinerant seller of pigeons
crying,
"Fat pigeons, pure pigeons, dove-white, slate grey,
living breathing pigeons
none of your reanimated muck here, sir."

I have pigeons and to spare and I tell him so.
He tells me he's new in this business,
used to be part of a moderately successful
financial securities analysis company
but was laid off, replaced by a computer RS232'd to a quartz sphere.
"Still, mustn't grumble, one door opens another one slams
got to keep up with the times sir, got to keep up with the times."
He thrusts me a free pigeon
(to attract new custom, sir,
once you've tried one of our pigeons you'll never look at another)
and struts down the stairs singing
"Pigeons alive-oh, alive alive-oh."

Ten o'clock after I've bathed and shaved
(unguents of eternal youth and of certain sexual attraction applied from plastic
vessels)
I take the pigeon into my study;

Angels and Visitations

I refresh the chalk circle around my old Dell 310,
hang wards at each corner of the monitor,

and do what is needful with the pigeon.

Then I turn the computer to on: it chugs and hums,
inside it fans blow like stormwinds on old oceans
ready to drown poor merchantmen,
Autoexec complete it bleeps:
I'll do, I'll do, I'll do...

II.

Two o'clock and walking through familiar London
—Or what was familiar London before the cursor deleted certain certainties—
I watch a suit and tie man giving suck
to the Psion Organiser lodged in his breast pocket
its serial interface like a cool mouth hunting his chest for sustenance,
familiar feeling, and I'm watching my breath steam in the air.

Cold as a witch's tit these days is London,
you'd never think it was November,
and from underground the sounds of trains rumble.
Mysterious: tube trains are almost legendary in these times,
stopping only for virgins and the pure of heart,
first stop Avalon, Lyonesse, or the Isles of the Blessed. Maybe
you get a postcard and maybe you don't.
Anyway, looking down any chasm demonstrates conclusively
there is no room under London for subways;
I warm my hands at a pit.
Flames lick upward.

Far below a smiling demon spots me, waves, mouths carefully,
as one does to the deaf, or distant, or to foreigners:

its sales performance is spotless: it mimes a Dwarrow Clone,
mimes software beyond my wildest,
Albertus Magnus ARChived on three floppies,
Claviculae Solomon for VGA, CGA, four-colour or monochrome,
mimes
and mimes
and mimes.

The tourists lean over the riftways to Hell
staring at the damned
(perhaps the worst part of damnation;
eternal torture is bearable in noble silence, alone
but an audience, eating crisps and chips and chestnuts,
an audience who aren't even really that interested...
They must feel like something at the zoo,
the damned).

Pigeons flutter around hell, dancing on the updrafts,
race memory perhaps telling them
that somewhere around here there should be four lions,
unfrozen water, one stone man above;
the tourists cluster around.
One does a deal with the demon: a ten-pack of blank floppies for his soul.
One has recognised a relative in the flames and is waving:
    Coooee! Coooeee! Uncle Joseph! Look, Nerissa, it's your Great-Uncle Joe
    that died before you was born,
      that's him down there, in the Slough, up to his eyes in boiling scum
      with the worms crawling in and out of his face.
    Such a lovely man.
    We all cried at his funeral.
    Wave to your uncle, Nerissa, wave to your uncle.

The pigeon man lays limed twigs on the cracked paving stones,
then sprinkles breadcrumbs and waits.

Angels and Visitations

He raises his cap to me.
"This morning's pigeon, sir, I trust it was satisfactory?"
I allow that it was, and toss him a golden shilling,
(which he touches surreptitiously to the iron of his gauntlet,
checking for fairy gold, then palms).

Tuesdays, I tell him. Come on Tuesdays.

III.

Birdlegged cottages and huts crowd the London streets,
stepping spindly over the taxis, shitting embers over cyclists,
queuing in the streets behind the busses,
chuckchuckchuckchuckchuurck, they murmur.
Old women with iron teeth gaze out of the windows
then return to their magic mirrors,
or to their housework,
Hoovering through fog and filthy air.

IV.

Four o'clock in Old Soho,
rapidly becoming a backwater of lost technology.
The ratcheting grate of charms being wound up
with clockwork silver keys
grinds out from every backstreet Watchmaker's,
Abortionist's, Philtre & Tobacconist's.

It's raining.

Bulletin board kids drive pimpmobiles in floppy hats,
modem panders
anoracked kid-kings of signal to noise;
and all their neon-lit stippled stable flirting and turning under the lights,

76

succubi and incubi with sell-by dates and Smart Card eyes,
all yours, if you've got your number,
know your expiry date, all that.
One of them winks at me
(flashes on, on-off, off-off-on),
noise swallows signal in fumbled fellatio.
(I cross two fingers,
a binary precaution against hex,
effective as superconductor or simple superstition.)
Two poltergeists share a take-away. Old Soho always makes me
nervous.

Brewer Street. A hiss from an alley: Mephistopheles opens his brown coat,
flashes me the lining (databased old invocations,
Magians lay ghosts — with diagrams), curses, and begins:
— Blight an enemy?
   Wither a harvest?
   Barren a consort?
   Debase an innocent?
   Ruin a party...?
   For you, sir? No, sir? Reconsider I beg you. Just a little of your blood
smudged on this printout
and you can be the proud possessor of a new voice-synthesiser, listen —

He stands a Zenith portable on a table he makes from a modest suitcase,
attracting a small audience in the process, plugs in the voicebox,
types at the
C> prompt: GO
and it recites in voice exact and fine —
*orientis princeps Beelzebub, inferni irredentista menarche et demigorgon,
propitiamus vows —*

77

Angels and Visitations

I hurry onwards, hurry down the street
while paper ghosts, old printouts, dog my heels,
and hear him patter like a market man:
— Not twenty
    Not eighteen
    Not fifteen,
    Cost me twelve lady so help me Satan but to you?
    Because I like your pretty face
    Because I want to raise your spirits

    Five.
    That's right.

    Five.

Sold to the lady with the lovely eyes...

V.

The Archbishop hunches glaucous blind in the darkness on the edge of St Paul's,
small, birdlike, luminous, humming *I/O, I/O, I/O.*
It's almost six and the rush hour traffic in stolen dreams
and expanded memory hustles the pavement below us.

I hand the man my jug.
He takes it, carefully, and shuffles back into the waiting cathedral shadows.
When he returns the jug is full once more.
I josh, "Guaranteed holy?"
He traces one word in the frozen dirt: *WYSIWYG,*
and does not smile back.

(Wheezy wig. Whisky whig.)
He coughs grey, milk-phlegm,
spits onto the steps.

What I see in the jug: it looks holy enough, but you can't know for sure,
not unless you are yourself a siren or a fetch,
coagulating out of a telecom mouthpiece, riding the bleep,
an invocation, some really Wrong Number; then you can tell
from holy.
I've dumped telephones in buckets of the stuff before now,
watched things begin to form
then bubble and hiss as the water gets to them:
lustrated and asperged, the Final Sanction.
One afternoon
there was a queue of them, trapped on the tape of my ansaphone:
I copied it to floppy and filed it away.
You want it?
Listen, everything's for sale.

The priest needs shaving, and he's got the shakes.
His wine-stained vestments do little to keep him warm.
I give him money.
(Not much. After all,
it's just water, some creatures are so stupid
they'll do you a Savini gunk-dissolve
if you sprinkle them with Perrier
for chrissakes, whining the whole time
All my evil, my beautiful evil.)

The old priest pockets the coin, gives me
a bag of crumbs as a bonus,
sits on his steps hugging himself.

I feel the need to say something before I leave.
Look, I tell him, it's not your fault.
It's just a multi-user system.
You weren't to know.
If prayers could be networked,

if saintware were up and running,
if you could make your side as reliable as they've made theirs....

"What You See," he mutters desolately,
"What You See Is What You Get." He crumbles a communion wafer
throws it down for the pigeons,
makes no attempt to catch even the slowest bird.

Cold wars produce bad losers.
I go home.

VI.

News at Ten. And here is Abel Drugger reading it:

VII.

The corners of my eyes catch hasty, bloodless motion —
a mouse?
Well, certainly a peripheral of some kind.

VIII.

It's bed-time. I feed the pigeons,
then undress.
Contemplate downloading a succubus from a board,
maybe just call up a sidekick,
(there's public domain stuff, bawds and bauds,
shareware, no need to pay a fortune,
even copy-protected stuff can be copied, passed about,
everything has a price, any of us).
Dryware, wetware, hardware, software,
blackware, darkware,
nightware, nightmare...

The modem sits inviting beside the phone,
red eyes.
I let it rest —
you can't trust anybody these days.
You download, hell, you don't know where what came from anymore,
who had it last.
Well, aren't you? Aren't you scared of viruses?
Even the better protected files corrupt,
and the best protected corrupt absolutely.

In the kitchen I hear the pigeons billing and queuing,
dreaming of left-handed knives,
of athanors and mirrors.

Pigeon blood stains the floor of my study.

Alone, I sleep. And all alone I dream.

IX.

Perhaps I wake in the night, suddenly comprehending something,
reach out,
scribble on the back of an old bill
my revelation, my newfound understanding,
knowing that morning will render it prosaic,
knowing that magic is a night-time thing,
then remembering when it still was...
Revelation retreats to cliché, listen:
    Things seemed simpler before we kept computers.

X.

Waking or dreaming from outside I hear
wild sabbats, screaming winds, tape hum, metal machine music;

Angels and Visitations

witches astride ghetto blasters crowd the moon,
then land on the heath their naked flanks aglisten.
No-one pays anything to attend the meet, each has it taken care of in advance,
baby bones with fat still clinging to them;
these things are direct debit, standing order,
and I see
    or think I see
a face I recognise and all of them queue up to kiss his arse,
let's rim the Devil, boys, cold seed,
and in the dark he turns and looks at me:
  — One door opens another one slams,
    I trust that everything is satisfactory?
    We do what we can, everybody's got the right to turn an honest penny:
    we're all bankrupt, sir,
    we're all redundant,
    but we make the best of it, whistle through the Blitz,
    that's the business. Fair trade is no robbery.
    Tuesday morning, then, sir, with the pigeons?

I nod and draw the curtains. Junk mail is everywhere.
They'll get to you,
one way or another they'll get to you; some day
I'll find my tube train underground, I'll pay no fare,
just "this is hell, and I want out of it,"
and then things will be simple once again.

It will come for me like a dragon down a dark tunnel.

LUTHER'S VILLANELLE

I get the feeling I've been here before
(Which is of course unlikely to be true)
But in these times it's so hard to be sure...

Consider the cold bastions of law
The clunk of padlock, muttered curse of screw —
I get the feeling I've been here before.

A thousand worlds and every world's a door.
The lights go out; I think I think of you,
But in these times it's so hard to be sure.

There's black blood slowly clotting on the floor,
Adhering to the bottom of my shoe.
I get the feeling I've been here before.

I've never been intentionally obscure,
I've never been intentionally taboo,
But in these times it's so hard to be sure.

There is no crime, though somewhere there's a clue.
Not far away the game begins anew...
But in these times it's so hard to be sure:
I get the feeling I've been here before.

MOUSE

THEY HAD a number of devices that would kill the mouse fast, others that would kill it more slowly. There were a dozen variants on the traditional mousetrap, the one Regan tended to think of as a Tom & Jerry trap: a metal spring trap that would slam down at a touch, breaking the mouse's back; there were other gadgets on the shelves — ones that suffocated the mouse, others that electrocuted it, or even drowned it, each safe in its multicoloured cardboard package.

"These weren't quite what I was looking for," said Regan.

"Well, that's all we got in the way of traps," said the woman, who wore a large plastic name-tag that said her name was *BECKY* and that she *Loves Working FOR YOU at MacRea's Animal Feed and Specialty Store*. "Now, over here —"

She pointed to a stand-alone display of *HUN-GREE-CAT MOUSE POISON* sachets. A little rubber mouse lay on the top of the display, his legs in the air.

Regan experienced a sudden memory flash, unbidden: Gwen, extending an elegant pink hand, her fingers curled upward. "What's that?" she said. It was the week before he had left for America.

"I don't know," said Regan. They were in the bar of a small hotel in the West Country, burgundy-coloured carpets, fawn-coloured wallpaper. He was nursing a gin and tonic, she was sipping her second glass of Chablis. Gwen had once told Regan that blondes should only drink white wine — it looked better. He laughed, until he realised she meant it.

"It's a dead one of *these*," she said, turning her hand over, so the fingers hung like the legs of a slow pink animal. He smiled. Later he paid the bill, and they went upstairs to Regan's room...

"No. Not poison. You see, I don't want to kill it," he told the saleswoman, Becky.

She looked at him curiously, as if he had just begun to speak in a foreign tongue. "But you said you wanted mousetraps...?"

"Look, what I want is a humane trap. It's like a corridor. The mouse goes in, the door shuts behind it, it can't get out."

"So how do you kill it?"

"You don't kill it. You drive a few miles away and let it go. And it doesn't come back to bother you."

Becky was smiling now, examining him as if he were just the most darling thing, just the sweetest, dumbest, cutest little thing. "You stay here," she said. "I'll check out back."

She walked through a door marked Employees Only. She had a nice bottom, thought Regan, and was sort of attractive, in a dull Midwestern sort of way.

He glanced out the window. Janice was sitting in the car, reading her magazine: a red-haired woman in a dowdy housecoat. He waved at her, but she wasn't looking at him.

Becky put her head back through the doorway. "Jackpot!" she said. "How many you want?"

"Two?"

"No problem." She was gone again, and returned with two small green plastic containers. She rang them up on the till, and as he fumbled through his notes and coins, still unfamiliar, trying to put together the correct change, she examined the traps, smiling, turning the packets over in her hands.

"My lord," she said. "Whatever will they think of next?"

The heat slammed Regan as he stepped out of the store.

He hurried over to the car. The metal door handle was hot in his hand; the engine was idling.

He climbed in. "I got two," he said. The air-conditioning in the car was cool and pleasant.

"Seatbelt on," said Janice. "You really got to learn to drive over here." She put down her magazine.

"I will," he said. "Eventually."

Regan was scared of driving in America: it was like driving on the other side of a mirror.

They said nothing else, and Regan read the instructions on the back of the mousetrap boxes. According to the text, the main attraction of this type of trap was that you never needed to see, touch, or handle the mouse. The door would close behind it, and that would be that. The instructions said nothing about not killing the mouse.

When they got home he took the traps out of the boxes, put a little peanut butter in one, down at the far end, a lump of cooking chocolate in the other, and placed them on the floor of the pantry, one against the wall, the other near the hole that the mice seemed to be using to gain access to the pantry.

The traps were only corridors. A door at one end, a wall at the other.

§　§　§

In bed that night, Regan reached out and touched Janice's breasts as she slept; touched them gently, not wanting to wake her. They were perceptibly fuller. He wished he found large breasts erotic. He found himself wondering what it must be like to suck a woman's breasts while she was lactating. He could imagine sweetness, but no specific taste.

Janice was sound asleep, but still she moved toward him.

He edged away; lay there in the dark, trying to remember how to sleep, hunting through alternatives in his mind. It was so hot, so stuffy. When they'd lived in Ealing he'd fallen asleep instantly, he was certain.

There was a sharp scream from the garden. Janice stirred and rolled away from him. It had sounded almost human. Foxes can sound like small children in pain — Regan had heard this long ago. Or perhaps it was a cat. Or a nightbird of some kind.

Something had died, anyway, in the night. Of that there was no doubt at all.

§　§　§

The next morning one of the traps had been sprung, although when Regan opened it, carefully, it proved to be empty. The chocolate bait had been nibbled. He opened the door to the trap once more and replaced it by the wall.

Janice was crying to herself in the lounge. Regan stood beside her; she reached out her hand, and he held it, tightly. Her fingers were cold. She was still wearing her nightgown, and she had put on no makeup.

Later, she made a telephone call.

A package arrived for Regan shortly before noon, by Federal Express, containing a dozen floppy disks; each filled with numbers for Regan to inspect and sort and classify.

He worked at the computer until six, sitting in front of a small metal fan which whirred and rattled, and moved the hot air around.

§   §   §

He turned on the radio that evening, while he cooked.

"...what my book *tells* everyone. What the liberals don't *want* us to know." The voice was high, nervous, arrogant.

"Yeah. Some of it was, well, kinda hard to believe." The host was encouraging; a deep radio voice, reassuring and easy on the ears.

"Of *course* it's hard to believe. It runs against everything they *want* you to believe. The liberals and the how-mo-sexuals in the media, they don't *let* you know the truth."

"Well, we all know that, friend. We'll be right back after this song."

It was a Country and Western song. Regan kept the radio tuned to the local National Public Radio station; sometimes they broadcast the BBC World Service News. Someone must have retuned it, he supposed, although he couldn't imagine who.

He took a sharp knife and cut through the chicken breast with care, parting the pink flesh, slicing it into strips all ready to stir-fry, listening to the song.

Somebody's heart was broken; somebody no longer cared. The song ended. There was a commercial for beer. Then the men began to talk again.

"Thing is, nobody believes it at first. But I got the *documents*. I got the *photographs*. You read my book. *You'll* see. It's the unholy alliance, and I *do* mean unholy, between the so called pro-choice lobby, the medical community and the how-mo-sexuals. The how-mos *need* these murders because that's where they get the little children they use to experiment with to find a cure for AIDS.

"I mean, those liberals talk about *Nazi* atrocities, but nothing those Nazis did comes in even *close* to what *they're* doing even as we speak. They take these human foetuses and they graft them onto little mice, to create these human-mouse hybrid creatures for their experiments. *Then* they inject them with AIDS..."

Regan found himself thinking of Mengele's wall of strung eyeballs. Blue eyes and brown eyes and hazel...

"Shit!" He'd sliced into his thumb. He pushed it into his mouth, bit down on it to stop the bleeding, ran into the bathroom and began to hunt for a band-aid.

"Remember, I'll need to be out of the house by ten tomorrow." Janice was standing behind him. He looked at her blue eyes in the bathroom mirror. She looked calm.

"Fine." He pulled the band-aid onto his thumb, hiding and binding the wound, and turned to face her.

"I saw a cat in the garden today," she said. "A big grey one. Maybe it's a stray."

"Maybe."

"Did you think any more about getting a pet?"

"Not really. It'd just be something else to worry about. I thought we agreed, no pets."

She shrugged.

They went back into the kitchen. He poured oil into the frying pan, and lit the gas. He dropped the strips of pink flesh into the pan and watched them shrink and discolour and change.

§ § §

Janice drove herself to the bus station early the next morning. It was a long drive into the city, and she'd be in no condition to drive when she was ready to return. She took five hundred dollars with her, in cash.

Regan checked the traps. Neither of them had been touched. Then he prowled the corridors of the house.

Eventually, he phoned Gwen. The first time he misdialled, his fingers slipping on the buttons of the phone, the long string of digits confusing him. He tried again.

A ringing, then her voice on the line. "Allied Accountancy Associates. Good afternoon."

"Gwenny? It's me."

"Regan? It's you, isn't it? I was hoping you'd call eventually. I missed you." Her voice was distant; transatlantic crackle and hum taking her further away from him.

"It's expensive."

"Any more thoughts about coming back?"

"I don't know."

"So how's wifeykins?"

"Janice is...." He paused. Sighed. "Janice is just fine."

"I've started fucking our new sales director," said Gwen. "After your time. You don't know him. You've been gone for six months now. I mean, what's a girl to do?"

It occurred then to Regan that that was what he hated most about women: their practicality. Gwen had always made him use a condom, although he disliked condoms, while she had also used a diaphragm and a spermicide. Regan felt that somewhere in all there a level of spontaneity, of romance, of passion, was lost. He liked sex to be something that just happened, half in his head, half out of it. Something sudden and dirty and powerful.

His forehead began to throb.

"So what's the weather like out there?" Gwen asked, brightly.

"It's hot," said Regan.

"Wish it was here. It's been raining for weeks."

He said something about it being lovely to hear her voice again. Then he put the phone down.

Angels and Visitations

§   §   §

Regan checked the traps. Still empty.

He wandered into his office and flipped on the TV.

"...this is a little one. That's what *foetus* means. And one day she'll grow up to be a big one. She's got little fingers, little toes — she's even got little toenails."

A picture on the screen: red and pulsing and indistinct.

It cut to a woman with a huge smile, cuddling a baby.

"Some little ones like her will grow up to be nurses, or teachers, or musicians. One day one of them may even be president."

Back to the pink thing, filling the screen.

"But *this* little one will never grow up to be a big one. She's going to be killed tomorrow. And her mother says it isn't murder."

He flipped channels until he found *I Love Lucy*, the perfect background nothing, then he turned on the computer and got down to work.

After two hours spent chasing an error of under a hundred dollars through seemingly endless columns of figures his head began to ache. He got up and walked into the garden.

He missed having a garden; missed proper English lawns, with proper English grass. The grass out here was withered, brown and sparse, the trees bearded with spanish moss like a something from a science fiction movie. He followed a track out into the woods behind the house. Something grey and sleek slipped from behind one tree to another.

"Here, kitty kitty," called Regan. "Here puss puss puss."

He walked over to the tree and looked behind it. The cat, or whatever it had been, was gone.

Something stung his cheek. He slapped at it without thought, lowered his hand to find it stained with blood, a mosquito, half-squashed, still twitching in his palm.

He went back into the kitchen and poured himself a cup of coffee. He missed tea, but it just didn't taste the same out here.

§   §   §

Janice got home about six.

"How was it?"

She shrugged. "Fine."

"Yeah?"

"Yeah."

"I have to go back next week," she said. "For a checkup."

"To make sure they didn't leave any instruments inside you?"

"Whatever," she said.

"I've made a spaghetti bolognese," said Regan.

"I'm not hungry," said Janice. "I'm going to bed."

She went upstairs.

Regan worked until the numbers no longer added up. He went upstairs, and walked quietly into the darkened bedroom. He slipped off his clothes in the moonlight, dropped them onto the carpet and slid between the sheets.

He could feel Janice next to him. Her body was shaking, and the pillow was wet.

"Jan?"

She had her back to him.

"It was horrible," she whispered into her pillow. "It hurt so much. And they wouldn't give me a proper anaesthetic or anything. They said I could have a shot of Valium if I wanted one, but they didn't have an anaesthetist there any more. The lady said he couldn't stand the pressure and anyway it would have cost another two hundred dollars and nobody wanted to pay...

"It hurt so much." She was sobbing now, gasping the words as if they were being tugged out of her. "So much."

Regan got out of bed.

"Where are you going?"

"I don't have to listen to this," said Regan. "I really don't have to listen to this."

§   §   §

It was too hot in the house. Regan walked downstairs in only his underpants. He walked into the kitchen, bare feet making sticking noises on the vinyl.

One of the mousetrap doors was closed.

91

He picked up the trap. It felt a trifle heavier than before. He opened the door carefully, a little way. Two beady black eyes stared up at him. Light brown fur. He pushed the door shut again, and heard a scrabbling from inside the trap.

Now what?

He couldn't kill it. He couldn't kill anything.

The green mousetrap smelled acrid, and the bottom of it was sticky with mouse-piss. Regan carried it gingerly out into the garden.

A gentle breeze had sprung up. The moon was almost full. He knelt on the ground, placed the trap carefully on the dry grass.

He opened the door of the small green corridor.

"Run away," he whispered, feeling embarrassed at the sound of his voice in the open air. "Run away, little mouse."

The mouse didn't move. He could see its nose at the door of the trap.

"Come on," said Regan. Bright moonlight; he could see everything, sharply lit and shadowed, if lacking in colour.

He nudged the trap with his foot.

The mouse made a dash for it, then. It ran out from the trap, then stopped, turned, and began to hop into the woods.

Then it stopped again. The mouse looked up in Regan's direction. Regan was convinced that it was staring at him. It had tiny pink hands. Regan felt almost paternal, then. He smiled, wistfully.

A streak of grey in the night, and the mouse hung, struggling uselessly, from the mouth of a large grey cat, its eyes burning green in the night. Then the cat bounded into the undergrowth.

He thought briefly of pursuing the cat, of freeing the mouse from its jaws...

There was a sharp scream from woods; just a night-sound, but for a moment Regan thought it sounded almost human, like a woman in pain.

He threw the little plastic mousetrap as far from him as he could. He was hoping for a satisfying crash as it hit something, but it fell soundlessly in the bushes.

Then Regan walked back inside, and he closed the door of the house behind him.

GUMSHOE

PUNCH Book Review of Josiah Thompson's *Gumshoe*

I NEVER ACTUALLY WORKED for the old regime. But I can't see them behaving like that; I mean, I've heard that nice Mister Coren on Gardeners' Question Time, or whatever that programme is, ("Ah, this is the story about the lady in Luton with the ferrets down her knickers." "No, I'm afraid not." "Then it's Sir Geoffrey Howe?" "Hoohoo, that's the one,") and he always sounded very nice. Not a man who'd resort to cheap threats, at any rate.

Not like the current bunch.

One of them rings me up, says he wants a review. This week. Fair enough, I say, when this week? Tuesday, he says. That's tomorrow, I point out. He says yes, that's tomorrow. Tuesday.

What if I can't get it done in time? I ask, all innocent.

There's a pause at the other end of the line; you can hear him looking up at the Men in Black Suits in the *Punch* offices, and getting the nod.

Well, he says calmly, then we'd have a blank page. And we'd print your photograph on it. Possibly your address. And we'd tell the *Punch* readership exactly whose fault it was that they had a blank page this week.

I wouldn't be able to enter a dentist's waiting room ever again.

Right, I said. Tomorrow. Put down the phone and describe him out loud. One word. Rhymes with custard, almost.

Okay. Write a review.

Only trouble is, tidied the office last week. Know I had the book somewhere, been tripping over it for a month, called *Gumshoe,* by some American philosophy professor who gave it all up to become a private eye. Gold cover.

Unique. Put it somewhere safe. Tidied it up. Very careful. Somewhere. Somewhere tidy and safe. Probably on a bookshelf. One of the bookshelves, anyway.

Only other trouble is, awful lot of books in here. No problem, just look for the gold cover. Up there on the top of top shelf, climb on the desk, reach up, nearly overbalance, pull it out: *Great Sex*.

Bugger.

Wonder briefly whether *Punch* would notice if review of *Great Sex* arrived tomorrow morning. Men in Black Suits in *Punch* offices. Suspicious bulges in jacket pockets. No sense of humour...

Forget *Great Sex*.

Review *Gumshoe*. Remember the title, anyway. Can't go too far wrong if you remember the title.

Don't have the book of course. Just *Great Sex*, funny there being two books with gold covers, flip it open, hope it'll be *Gumshoe* when I look at the pages. It isn't. "She has a magnificent polished body, the globes of her buttocks round and smooth like summer fruit, her breasts high and proud."

Wonder what *kind* of summer fruit. Raspberries? Gooseberries?

Go and check with encyclopedia.

Discover that the gooseberry may be white, yellow, green or red, and may have a prickly, hairy or smooth surface. Doesn't say a word about whether it's a summer fruit or not. Expect Alan Coren knows about that kind of thing, what with Gardeners' Question Time and everything...

Doesn't say a lot for her buttocks.

Give up.

Decide to write review from memory. Fake it convincingly. Right. No problem. This philosophy professor, wants to be a private eye, name of, name of, anyway, he's written all these books on Kierkegaard or possibly it was Wittgenstein, one of that mob, honest to goodness philosophy professor, earns good money, married with children, gives it all up, becomes a San Francisco private dick.

Was vaguely expecting something tacky, like this book I read once, forget the title, *My Life as a Private Eye Including Fifteen Surefire Ways to Cheat on Your Spouse Without Getting Caught*, something like that, or else maybe subChandler stuff, "Dame walks into my office, figure that'd get Descartes to come up with a new Proposition, sent my pulse rate over the speed limit, buttocks like thrusting gooseberries," and was pleasantly surprised it's neither.

Not tacky.

Philosophy professor finds true happiness as penniless Sam Spade. Reads *The Maltese Falcon* a lot between cases. Good writer. Finds thirty thousand dollars of drug money under the floorboards of attic. Gets kidnapped child out of India. Tries to save fitted-up Oriental from electric chair. Or gas chamber. One of those. Forget my own head next. Decides detection is Real Life. Never happier. Photo on the cover of the book: crinkly eyes, good man in a tough spot, copy of *The Maltese Falcon* open on his lap.

Wish I could remember his name. Begins with L, or S. Or P, maybe.

Best sections are long, boring bits, sitting in cars waiting for people who never show, pissing into styrofoam cups. Convinced me I didn't want to be a private dick. Glad someone else is doing it, though.

Good private eye could find anything. Even copy of *Gumshoe* with gold cover. Probably look in most obvious place. Probably just sit down at desk, casual glance to the left, look over to stack of books writer's promised to review at some time or other...

Shit.

Gold cover.

Author's name Josiah Thompson. Book called *Gumshoe*, though; remembered that much. Says on the cover "The best book ever written about the life of the private eye."

I'd go along with that.

THE CASE OF THE
FOUR AND TWENTY BLACKBIRDS

I SAT in my office, nursing a glass of hooch and idly cleaning my automatic. Outside the rain fell steadily, like it seems to do most of the time in our fair city, whatever the tourist board says. Hell, I didn't care. I'm not on the tourist board. I'm a private dick, and one of the best, although you wouldn't have known it; the office was crumbling, the rent was unpaid and the hooch was my last.

Things are tough all over.

To cap it all the only client I'd had all week never showed up on the street corner where I'd waited for him. He said it was going to be a big job, but now I'd never know: he kept a prior appointment in the morgue.

So when the dame walked into my office I was sure my luck had changed for the better.

"What are you selling, lady?"

She gave me a look that would have induced heavy breathing in a pumpkin, and which shot my heartbeat up to three figures. She had long blonde hair and a figure that would have made Thomas Aquinas forget his vows. I forgot all mine about never taking cases from dames.

"What would you say to some of the green stuff?" she asked in a husky voice, getting straight to the point.

"Continue, sister." I didn't want her to know how bad I needed the dough, so I held my hand in front of my mouth; it doesn't help if a client sees you salivate.

She opened her purse and flipped out a photograph — a glossy eight by ten. "Do you recognise that man?"

In my business you know who people are. "Yeah."

"He's dead."

"I know that too, sweetheart. It's old news. It was an accident."

Her gaze went so icy you could have chipped it into cubes and cooled a cocktail with it. "My brother's death was no accident."

I raised an eyebrow — you need a lot of arcane skills in my business — and said "Your brother, eh?" Funny, she hadn't struck me as the type that had brothers.

"I'm Jill Dumpty."

"So your brother was Humpty Dumpty?"

"And he didn't fall off that wall, Mr Horner. He was pushed."

Interesting, if true. Dumpty had his finger in most of the crooked pies in town; I could think of five guys who would have preferred to see him dead than alive without trying.

Without trying too hard, anyway.

"You seen the cops about this?"

"Nah. The King's Men aren't interested in anything to do with his death. They say they did all they could do in trying to put him together again after the fall."

I leaned back in my chair.

"So what's it to you? Why do you need me?"

"I want you to find the killer, Mr Horner. I want him brought to justice. I want him to fry like an egg. Oh — and one other *little* thing," she added, lightly. "Before he died Humpty had a small manila envelope full of photographs he was meant to be sending me. Medical photos. I'm a trainee nurse, and I need them to pass my finals."

I inspected my nails, then looked up at her face, taking in a handful of waist and Easter-egg bazonkas on the way up. She was a looker, although her cute nose was a little on the shiny side. "I'll take the case. Seventy-five a day and two hundred bonus for results."

She smiled; my stomach twisted around once and went into orbit. "You get another two hundred if you get me those photographs. I want to be a nurse *real* bad." Then she dropped three fifties on my desktop.

I let a devil-may-care grin play across my rugged face. "Say, sister, how about letting me take you out for dinner? I just came into some money."

Angels and Visitations

She gave an involuntary shiver of anticipation and muttered something about having a thing about midgets, so I knew I was onto a good thing. Then she gave me a lopsided smile that would have made Albert Einstein drop a decimal point. "First find my brother's killer, Mr Horner. And my photographs. *Then* we can play."

She closed the door behind her. Maybe it was still raining but I didn't notice. I didn't care.

§   §   §

There are parts of town the tourist board don't mention. Parts of town where the police travel in threes if they travel at all. In my line of work you get to visit them more than is healthy. Healthy is never.

He was waiting for me outside Luigi's. I slid up behind him, my rubber-soled shoes soundless on the shiny wet sidewalk.

"Hiya, Cock."

He jumped and spun around; I found myself gazing up into the muzzle of a .45. "Oh, Horner." He put the gun away. "Don't call me Cock. I'm Bernie Robin to you, Short-stuff, and don't you forget it."

"Cock Robin is good enough for me, Cock. Who killed Humpty Dumpty?"

He was a strange-looking bird, but you can't be choosy in my profession. He was the best underworld lead I had.

"Let's see the colour of your money."

I showed him a fifty.

"Hell," he muttered. "It's green. Why can't they make puce or mauve money for a change?" He took it, though. "All I know is that the Fat Man had his finger in a lot of pies."

"So?"

"One of those pies had four and twenty blackbirds in it."

"Huh?"

"Do I hafta spell it out for you? I... *Ughh*..." He crumpled to the sidewalk, an arrow protruding from his back. Cock Robin wasn't going to be doing any more chirping.

The Case of the Four and Twenty Blackbirds

§   §   §

Sergeant O'Grady looked down at the body, then he looked down at me. "Faith and begorrah, to be sure," he said. "If it isn't Little Jack Horner himself."

"I didn't kill Cock Robin, Sarge."

"And I suppose that the call we got down at the station telling us you were going to be rubbing the late Mr Robin out. Here. Tonight. Was just a hoax?"

"If I'm the killer, where are my arrows?" I thumbed open a pack of gum and started to chew. "It's a frame."

He puffed on his meerschaum and then put it away, and idly played a couple of phrases of the *William Tell Overture* on his oboe. "Maybe. Maybe not. But you're still a suspect. Don't leave town. And Horner..."

"Yeah?"

"Dumpty's death was an accident. That's what the coroner said. That's what I say. Drop the case."

I thought about it. Then I thought of the money, and the girl. "No dice, Sarge."

He shrugged. "It's your funeral." He said it like it probably would be.

I had a funny feeling like he could be right.

"You're out of your depth, Horner. You're playing with the big boys. And it ain't healthy."

From what I could remember of my schooldays he was correct. Whenever I played with the big boys I always wound up having the stuffing beaten out of me. But how did O'Grady — how *could* O'Grady have known that? Then I remembered something else.

O'Grady was the one that used to beat me up the most.

§   §   §

It was time for what we in the profession call "legwork". I made a few discreet enquiries around town, but found out nothing about Dumpty that I didn't know already.

99

The Case of the Four and Twenty Blackbirds

Humpty Dumpty was a bad egg. I remembered him when he was new in town, a smart young animal trainer with a nice line in training mice to run up clocks. He went to the bad pretty fast though; gambling, drink, women, it's the same story all over. A bright young kid thinks that the streets of Nurseryland are paved with gold, and by the time he finds out otherwise it's much too late.

Dumpty started off with extortions and robbery on a small scale — he trained up a team of spiders to scare little girls away from their curds and whey, which he'd pick up and sell on the black market. Then he moved onto blackmail — the nastiest game. We crossed paths once, when I was hired by this young society kid — let's call him Georgie Porgie — to recover some compromising snaps of him kissing the girls and making them cry. I got the snaps, but I learned it wasn't healthy to mess with the Fat Man. And I don't make the same mistakes twice. Hell, in my line of work I can't afford to make the same mistakes once.

It's a tough world out there. I remember when Little Bo Peep first came to town...but you don't want to hear my troubles. If you're not dead yet, you've got troubles of your own.

I checked out the newspaper files on Dumpty's death. One minute he was sitting on a wall, the next he was in pieces at the bottom. All the King's Horses and all the King's Men were on the scene in minutes, but he needed more than first aid. A medic named Foster was called — a friend of Dumpty's from his Gloucester days — although I don't know of anything a doc can do when you're dead.

Hang on a second — *Dr Foster!*

I got that old feeling you get in my line of work. Two little brain cells rub together the right way and in seconds you've got a twenty-four-carat cerebral fire on your hands.

You remember the client who didn't show — the one I'd waited for all day on the street corner? An accidental death. I hadn't bothered to check it out — I can't afford to waste time on clients who aren't going to pay for it.

Three deaths, it seemed. Not one.

I reached for the telephone and rang the police station. "This is Horner," I told the desk man. "Lemme speak to Sergeant O'Grady."

There was a crackling and he came on the line. "O'Grady speaking."

"It's Horner."

"Hi, Little Jack." That was just like O'Grady. He'd been kidding me about my size since we were kids together. "You finally figured out that Dumpty's death was an accident?"

"Nope. I'm now investigating three deaths. The Fat Man's, Bernie Robin's and Dr Foster's."

"Foster the plastic surgeon? His death was an accident."

"Sure. And your mother was married to your father."

There was a pause. "Horner, if you phoned me up just to talk dirty, I'm not amused."

"Okay, wise guy. If Humpty Dumpty's death was an accident and so was Dr Foster's, tell me just one thing.

"Who killed Cock Robin?"

I don't ever get accused of having too much imagination, but there's one thing I'd swear to. I could *hear* him grinning over the phone as he said: "You did, Horner. And I'm staking my badge on it."

The line went dead.

§　　　§　　　§

My office was cold and lonely, so I wandered down to Joe's Bar for some companionship and a drink or three.

Four and twenty blackbirds. A dead doctor. The Fat Man. Cock Robin...Heck, this case had more holes in it than a Swiss cheese and more loose ends than a torn string vest. And where did the juicy Miss Dumpty come into it? Jack and Jill — we'd make a great team. When this was all over perhaps we could go off together to Louie's little place on the hill, where no-one's interested in whether you got a marriage license or not. "The Pail of Water", that was the name of the joint.

I called over the bartender. "Hey. Joe."

"Yeah, Mr Horner?" He was polishing a glass with a rag that had seen better days as a shirt.

"Did you ever meet the Fat Man's sister?"

He scratched at his cheek. "Can't say as I did. His sister...huh? Hey — the Fat Man didn't have a sister."

"You sure of that?"

"Sure I'm sure. It was the day my sister had her first kid — I told the Fat Man I was an uncle. He gave me this look and says, 'Ain't no way I'll ever be an uncle, Joe. Got no sisters or brother, nor no other kinfolk neither.'"

If the mysterious Miss Dumpty wasn't his sister, who *was* she?

"Tell me, Joe. Didja ever see him in here with a dame — about so high, shaped like this?" My hands described a couple of parabolas. "Looks like a blonde love goddess."

He shook his head. "Never saw him with any dames. Recently he was hanging around with some medical guy, but the only thing he ever cared about was those crazy birds and animals of his."

I took a swig of my drink. It nearly took the roof of my mouth off. "Animals? I thought he'd given all that up."

"Naw — couple weeks back he was in here with a whole bunch of black-birds he was training to sing 'Wasn't that a dainty dish to set before *Mmm Mmm*.'"

"*Mmm Mmm*?"

"Yeah. I got no idea who."

I put my drink down. A little of it spilt on the counter, and I watched it strip the varnish. "Thanks, Joe. You've been a big help." I handed him a ten dollar bill. "For information received,' I said, adding, "Don't spend it all at once."

In my profession it's making little jokes like that that keeps you sane.

§　　　§　　　§

I had one contact left. I found a pay phone and called her number.

"Old Mother Hubbard's Cupboard — Cake Shop and Licensed Soup Kitchen."

"It's Horner, Ma."

"Jack? It ain't safe for me to talk to you."

"For old time's sake, sweetheart. You owe me a favour." Some two-bit crooks had once knocked off the Cupboard, leaving it bare. I'd tracked them down and returned the cakes and soup.

"...Okay. But I don't like it."

"*You* know everything that goes on around here on the food front, Ma. What's the significance of a pie with four and twenty trained blackbirds in it?"

She whistled, long and low. "You really don't know?"

"I wouldn't be asking you if I did."

"You should read the Court pages of the papers next time, sugar. Jeez. You are out of your depth."

"C'mon, Ma. Spill it."

"It so happens that that particular dish was set before the King a few weeks back....Jack? Are you still there?"

"I'm still here ma'am." I said, quietly. "All of a sudden a lot of things are starting to make sense." I put down the phone.

It was beginning to look like Little Jack Horner had pulled out a plum from this pie.

It was raining, steady and cold.

I phoned a cab.

Quarter of an hour later one lurched out of the darkness.

"You're late."

"So complain to the tourist board."

I climbed in the back, wound down the window, and lit a cigarette.

And I went to see the Queen.

§ § §

The door to the private part of the palace was locked. It's the part that the public don't get to see. But I've never been public, and the little lock hardly slowed me up. The door to the private apartments with the big red heart on it was unlocked, so I knocked and walked straight in.

The Queen of Hearts was alone, standing in front of the mirror, holding a plate of jam tarts with one hand, powdering her nose with the other. She turned, saw me, and gasped, dropping the tarts.

104

"Hey, Queenie," I said. "Or would you feel more comfortable if I called you Jill?"

She was still a good-looking slice of dame, even without the blonde wig.

"Get out of here!" she hissed.

"I don't think so, toots." I sat down on the bed. "Let me spell a few things out for you."

"Go ahead." She reached behind her for a concealed alarm button. I let her press it. I'd cut the wires on my way in — in my profession there's no such thing as being too careful.

"Let me spell a few things out for you."

"You just said that."

"I'll tell this my way, lady."

I lit a cigarette and a thin plume of blue smoke drifted heavenwards, which was where I was going if my hunch was wrong. Still, I've learned to trust hunches.

"Try this on for size. Dumpty — the Fat Man — wasn't your brother. He wasn't even your friend. In fact he was blackmailing you. He knew about your nose."

She turned whiter than a number of corpses I've met in my time in the business. Her hand reached up and cradled her freshly powdered nose.

"You see, I've known the Fat Man for many years, and many years ago he had a lucrative concern in training animals and birds to do certain unsavoury things. And that got me to thinking... I had a client recently who didn't show, due to his having been stiffed first. Doctor Foster, of Gloucester, the plastic surgeon. The official version of his death was that he'd just sat too close to a fire and melted.

"But just suppose he was killed to stop him telling something that he knew? I put two and two together and hit the jackpot. Let me reconstruct a scene for you: You were out in the garden — probably hanging out some clothes — when along came one of Dumpty's trained pie-blackbirds and *pecked off your nose.*

"So there you were, standing in the garden, your hand in front of your face, when along comes the Fat Man with an offer you couldn't refuse. He could introduce you to a plastic surgeon who could fix you up with a nose as good as new, for a price. And no-one need ever know. Am I right so far?"

She nodded dumbly, then finding her voice, muttered: "Pretty much. But I ran back into the parlour after the attack, to eat some bread and honey. That was where he found me."

"Fair enough." The colour was starting to come back into her cheeks now. "So you had the operation from Foster, and no-one was going to be any the wiser. Until Dumpty told you that he had photos of the op. You had to get rid of him. A couple of days later you were out walking in the palace grounds. There was Humpty, sitting on a wall, his back to you, gazing out into the distance. In a fit of madness, you pushed. And Humpty Dumpty had a great fall.

"But now you were in big trouble. Nobody suspected you of his murder, but where were the photographs? Foster didn't have them, although he smelled a rat and had to be disposed of — before he could see me. But you didn't know how much he'd told me, and you still didn't have the snapshots, so you took me on to find out. And that was your mistake, sister."

Her lower lip trembled, and my heart quivered. "You won't turn me in, will you?"

"Sister, you tried to frame me this afternoon. I don't take kindly to that."

With a shaking hand she started to unbutton her blouse. "Perhaps we could come to some sort of arrangement?"

I shook my head. "Sorry, Your Majesty. Mrs Horner's little boy Jack was always taught to keep his hands off royalty. It's a pity, but that's how it is." To be on the safe side I looked away, which was a mistake. A cute little ladies' pistol was in her hands and pointing at me before you could sing a song of sixpence. The shooter may have been small, but I knew it packed enough of a wallop to take me out of the game permanently.

This dame was *lethal*.

"Put that gun down, Your Majesty." Sergeant O'Grady strolled through the bedroom door, his police special clutched in his ham-like fist.

"I'm sorry I suspected you, Horner," he said drily. "You're lucky I did, though, sure and begorrah. I had you trailed here and I overheard the whole thing."

"Hi, Sarge, thanks for stopping by. But I hadn't finished my explanation. If you'll take a seat I'll wrap it up."

He nodded brusquely, and sat down near the door. His gun hardly moved.

I got up from the bed and walked over to the Queen. "You see, Toots, what I didn't tell you was who did *have* the snaps of your nose job. Humpty did, when you killed him."

A charming frown crinkled her perfect brow. "I don't understand... I had the body searched."

"Sure, afterwards. But the first people to get to the Fat Man were the King's Men. The cops. And one of them pocketed the envelope. When any fuss had died down the blackmail would have started again. Only this time you wouldn't have known who to kill. And I owe you an apology." I bent down to tie my shoelaces.

"Why?"

"I accused you of trying to frame me this afternoon. You didn't. That arrow was the property of a boy who was the best archer in my school — I should have recognised that distinctive fletching anywhere. Isn't that right," I said, turning back to the door, "...'Sparrow' O'Grady?"

Under the guise of tying up my shoelaces I had already palmed a couple of the Queen's jam tarts, and, flinging one of them upwards, I neatly smashed the room's only light bulb.

It only delayed the shooting a few seconds, but a few seconds was all I needed, and as the Queen of Hearts and Sergeant 'Sparrow' O'Grady cheerfully shot each other to bits, I split.

In my business, you have to look after number one.

Munching on a jam tart I walked out of the palace grounds and into the street. I paused by a trash-can, to try to burn the manila envelope of photographs I had pulled from O'Grady's pocket as I walked past him, but it was raining so hard they wouldn't catch.

When I got back to my office I phoned the tourist board to complain. They said the rain was good for the farmers, and I told them what they could do with it.

They said that things are tough all over.

And I said. Yeah.

VIRUS

There was a computer game, I was given it,
one of my friends gave it to me, he was playing it,
he said, it's brilliant, you should play it,
and I did, and it was.

I copied it off the disk he gave me
for anyone, I wanted everyone to play it.
Everyone should have this much fun.
I sent it upline to bulletin boards
but mainly I got it out to all of my friends.

(Personal contact. That's the way it was given to me.)

My friends were like me: some were scared of viruses,
someone gave you a game on disk, next week or Friday the 13th
it reformatted your hard disk or corrupted your memory.
But this one never did that. This was dead safe.

Even my friends who didn't like computers started to play:
as you get better the game gets harder;
maybe you never win but you can get pretty good.
I'm pretty good.

Of course I have to spend a lot of time playing it.
So do my friends. And their friends.
And just the people you meet, you can see them,

108

walking down the old motorways
or standing in queues, away from their computers,
away from the arcades that sprang up overnight,
but they play it in their heads in the meantime,
combining shapes,
puzzling over contours, putting colours next to colours,
twisting signals to new screen sections,
listening to the music.

Sure, people think about it, but mainly they play it.
My record's eighteen hours at a stretch.
40,012 points, 3 fanfares.

You play through the tears, the aching wrist, the hunger, after a while
it all goes away.
All of it except the game, I should say.

There's no room in my mind any more; no room for other things.
We copied the game, gave it to our friends.
It transcends language, occupies our time,
sometimes I think I'm forgetting things these days.

I wonder what happened to the TV. There used to be TV.
I wonder what will happen when I run out of canned food.
I wonder where all the people went. And then I realise how,
if I'm fast enough, I can put a black square next to a red line,
mirror it and rotate them so they both disappear,
clearing the left block
for a white bubble to rise...

(So they both disappear.)

And when the power goes off for good then I
Will play it in my head until I die.

LOOKING FOR THE GIRL

I WAS nineteen in 1965, in my drainpipe trousers with my hair quietly creeping down towards my collar. Every time you turned on the radio the Beatles were singing *Help!* and I wanted to be John Lennon with all the girls screaming after me, always ready with a cynical quip. That was the year I bought my first copy of *Penthouse* from a small tobacconist's in the King's Road. I paid my few furtive shillings, and went home with it stuffed up my jumper, occasionally glancing down to see if it had burnt a hole in the fabric.

The copy has long since been thrown away, but I'll always remember it: sedate letters about censorship; a short story by H. E. Bates and an interview with an American novelist I had never heard of; a fashion spread of mohair suits and paisley ties, all to be bought on Carnaby Street. And best of all, there were girls, of course; and best of all the girls there was Charlotte.

Charlotte was nineteen too.

All the girls in that long-gone magazine seemed identical, with their perfect plastic flesh; not a hair out of place (you could almost smell the lacquer); smiling wholesomely at the camera while their eyes squinted at you through forest-thick eyelashes: white lipstick; white teeth; white breasts, bikini-bleached. I never gave a thought to the strange positions they had coyly arranged themselves into to avoid showing the slightest curl or shadow of pubic hair — I wouldn't have known what I was looking at anyway. I had eyes only for their pale bottoms and breasts, their chaste but inviting come-on glances.

Then I turned the page, and I saw Charlotte. She was different from the others. Charlotte *was* sex; she wore sexuality like a translucent veil, like a heady perfume.

There were words beside the pictures and I read them in a daze. "The entrancing Charlotte Reave is nineteen...a resurgent individualist and beat poet, contributor to *FAB Magazine*..." Phrases stuck to my mind as I pored over the flat pictures: she posed and pouted in a Chelsea flat — the photographer's, I guessed — and I knew that I needed her.

She was my age. It was fate.

Charlotte.

Charlotte was nineteen.

I bought *Penthouse* regularly after that, hoping she'd appear again. But she didn't. Not then.

Six months later my mum found a shoebox under my bed, and looked inside it. First she threw a scene, then she threw out all the magazines, finally she threw me out. The next day I got a job and a bedsit in Earl's Court, without, all things considered, too much trouble.

The job, my first, was at an electrical shop off the Edgware Road. All I could do was change a plug, but in those days people could afford to get an electrician in to do just that. My boss told me I could learn on the job.

I lasted three weeks. My first job was a proper thrill — changing the plug on the bedside light of an English film-star, who had achieved fame through his portrayal of laconic, Cockney casanovas. When I got there he was in bed with two honest-to-goodness dolly-birds. I changed the plug and left — it was all very proper. I didn't even catch a glimpse of nipple, let alone get invited to join them.

Three weeks later I got fired and lost my virginity, on the same day. It was a posh place in Hampstead, empty apart from the maid, a little dark-haired woman, a few years older than me. I got down on my knees to change the plug, and she climbed on a chair next to me to dust off the top of a door. I looked up: under her skirt she was wearing stockings, and suspenders, and, so help me, nothing else. I discovered what happened in the bits the pictures didn't show you.

So I lost my cherry under a dining-room table in Hampstead. You don't see maidservants any more. They have gone the way of the bubble-car and the dinosaur.

It was afterwards that I lost my job. Not even my boss, convinced as he was of my utter incompetence, believed I could have taken three hours to change a plug—and I wasn't about to tell him that I'd spent two of the hours I'd been gone hiding underneath the dining-room table when the master and mistress of the house came home unexpectedly, was I?

I got a succession of short-lived jobs after that: first as a printer, then as a typesetter, before I wound up in a little ad agency above a sandwich shop in Old Compton Street.

I carried on buying *Penthouse*. Everybody looked like an extra in *The Avengers*, but they looked like that in real life. Articles on Woody Allen and Sappho's island, Batman and Vietnam, strippers in action wielding whips, fashion and fiction and sex.

The suits gained velvet collars, and the girls messed up their hair. Fetish was fashion. London was swinging, the magazine covers were psychedelic, and if there wasn't acid in the drinking water, we acted as if there ought to have been.

I saw Charlotte again in 1969, long after I'd given up on her. I thought that I had forgotten what she looked like. Then one day the head of the agency dropped a *Penthouse* on my desk — there was a cigarette ad we'd placed in it that he was particularly pleased with. I was twenty-three, a rising star, running the art department as if I knew what I was doing, and sometimes I did.

I don't remember much about the issue itself; all I remember is Charlotte. Hair wild and tawny, eyes provocative, smiling like she knew all the secrets of life, and she was keeping them close to her naked chest. Her name wasn't Charlotte then, it was Melanie, or something like that. The text said that she was nineteen.

I was living with a dancer called Rachel at the time, in a flat in Camden Town. She was the best-looking, most delightful woman I've ever known, was Rachel. And I went home early with those pictures of Charlotte in my brief-case, and locked myself in the bathroom, and I wanked myself into a daze.

We broke up shortly after that, me and Rachel.

The ad agency boomed — everything in the sixties' boomed — and in 1971 I was given the task of finding "The Face" for a clothing label. They wanted a girl who would epitomise everything sexual; who would wear their clothes as if she were about to reach up and rip them off, if some man didn't get there first. And I knew the perfect girl: Charlotte.

I phoned *Penthouse*, who didn't know what I was talking about, but, reluctantly, put me in touch with both of the photographers who had shot her in the past. The man at *Penthouse* didn't seen convinced when I told them it was the same girl each time.

I got hold of the photographers, trying to find her agency.

They said she didn't exist.

At least not in any way you could pin down, she didn't. Sure, both of them knew the girl I meant. But, as one of them told me, "like, *weird*", she'd come to them. They'd paid her a modelling fee and sold the pictures. No, they didn't have any addresses for her.

I was twenty-six, and a fool. I saw immediately what must be happening: I was being given the runaround. Some other ad agency had obviously signed her, was planning a big campaign around her, had paid the photographers to keep quiet. I cursed and I shouted at them, over the phone. I made outrageous financial offers.

They told me to fuck off.

And the next month she was in *Penthouse*. No longer a psychedelic tease mag, it had become classier — the girls had grown pubic hair, had man-eating glints in their eyes. Men and women romped in soft focus through cornfields, pink against the gold.

Her name, said the text, was Belinda. She was an antique dealer. It was Charlotte all right, although her hair was dark, and piled in rich ringlets over her head. The text also gave her age: nineteen.

I phoned my contact at *Penthouse* and got the name of the photographer, John Felbridge. I rang him. Like the others, he claimed to know nothing about her, but by now I'd learned a lesson. Instead of shouting at him down the telephone line, I gave him a job, on a fairly sizeable account, shooting a small boy eating ice-cream. Felbridge was long-haired, in his late thirties, with a ratty fur coat and plimsolls that were flapping open, but a good photographer. After the shoot I took him out for a drink, and we talked about the lousy weather, and photography, and decimal currency, and his previous work, and Charlotte.

"So you were saying you'd seen the pictures in *Penthouse*?" Felbridge said.

I nodded. We were both slightly drunk.

"I'll tell you about that girl. You know something? She's why I want to give up glamour work, and go legit. Said her name was Belinda."

"How did you meet her?"

"I'm getting to that aren't I? I thought she was from an agency, didn't I? She knocks on the door, I think strewth! and invite her in. She said she wasn't from an agency, she says she's selling..." He wrinkled his brow, confused, "...Isn't that odd? I've forgotten what she was selling. Maybe she wasn't selling anything. I don't know. I'll forget me own name next.

"I knew she was something special. Asked her if she'd pose, told her it was kosher, I wasn't just trying to get into her pants, and she agrees. Click, flash! Five rolls, just like that. As soon as we've finished she's got her clothes back on, heads out the door pretty-as-you-please. 'What about your money?' I says to her. 'Send it to me,' she says, and she's down the steps and onto the road."

"So you *have* got her address?" I asked, trying to keep the interest out of my voice.

"No. Bugger all. I wound up setting her fee aside in case she comes back."

I remember, in with the disappointment, wondering whether his cockney accent was real or merely fashionable.

"But what I was leading up to is this. When the pictures came back, I knew I'd...well, as far as tits and fanny went, no — as far as the whole photographing women thing went — I'd done it all. She *was* women, see? I'd *done* it. No, no, let me get you one. My shout. Bloody Mary, wasn't it? I gotter say, I'm looking forward to our future work together..."

There wasn't to be any future work.

The agency was taken over by an older, bigger firm, who wanted our accounts. They incorporated the initials of the firm into their own, and kept on a few top copywriters, but they let the rest of us go.

I went back to my flat and waited for the offers of work to pour in, which they didn't, but a friend of a girlfriend of a friend starting chatting to me late one night in a club (music by a guy I'd never heard of, name of David Bowie. He was dressed as a spaceman, the rest of his band were in silver cowboy outfits. I didn't even listen to the songs), and the next thing you know I was managing a rock band of my own, *The Diamonds of Flame*. Unless you were hanging around the London club scene in the early seventies you'll never have heard of them, although they were a very good band. Tight, lyrical. Five guys. Two of them are currently in world-league super groups. One of them's a plumber in Walsall; he still sends me Christmas cards. The other two have been dead for fifteen years: anonymous ODs. They went within a week of each other, and it broke up the band.

It broke me up, too. I dropped out after that — I wanted to get as far away from the city and that lifestyle as I could. I bought a small farm in Wales. I was happy there, too, with the sheep and the goats, and the cabbages. I'd probably be there today if it hadn't been for her, and *Penthouse*.

I don't know where it came from; one morning I went outside to find the magazine lying in the yard, in the mud, face-down. It was almost a year old. She wore no makeup, and was posed in what looked like a very high-class flat. For the first time I could see her pubic hair, or I could have if the photo hadn't been artistically fuzzed, and just a fraction out of focus. She looked as if she were coming out of the mist.

Her name, it said, was Lesley. She was nineteen.

And after that I just couldn't stay away any more. I sold the farm for a pittance, and came back to London in the last days of 1976.

I went on the dole, lived in a council flat in Victoria, got up at lunchtime, hit the pubs until they closed in the afternoons, read newspapers in the library until opening time, then pub-crawled until closing time. I lived off my dole money, and drank from my savings account.

I was thirty and I felt much older. I started living with an anonymous blonde punkette from Canada I met in a drinking club in Greek Street. She was the barmaid, and one night, after closing, she told me she'd just lost her digs, so I offered her the sofa at my place. She was only sixteen, it turned out, and she never got to sleep on the sofa. She had small, pomegranate breasts, a skull tattooed on her back, and a junior Bride of Frankenstein hairdo. She said she'd done everything, and believed in nothing. She would talk for hours about the way the world was moving toward a condition of anarchy, claimed that there was no hope, and no future; but she fucked like she'd just invented fucking. And I figured that was good.

She'd come to bed wearing nothing but a spiky black leather dog-collar, and masses of messy black eye-make-up. She spat sometimes, just gobbed on the pavement, when we were walking, which I hated, and she made me take her to the punk clubs, to watch her gob and swear and pogo. Then I really felt old. I liked some of the music, though: *Peaches*, stuff like that. And I saw the Sex Pistols play live. They were rotten.

Then the punkette walked out on me, claiming that I was a boring old fart and she took up with an extremely plump Arab princeling.

"I thought you didn't believe in anything," I called after her, as she climbed into the Roller he sent to collect her.

"I believe in £100 blowjobs, and mink sheets," she called back, one hand playing with a strand of her Bride of Frankenstein hairdo. "And a gold vibrator. I believe in that."

So she went away to an oil fortune and a new wardrobe, and I checked my savings and found I was dead broke — practically penniless. I was still sporadically buying *Penthouse*. My sixties soul was both deeply shocked and profoundly thrilled by the amount of flesh now on view. Nothing was left to the imagination, which, at the same time, attracted and repelled me.

Then, near the end of 1977, *she* was there again.

Her hair was multicoloured, my Charlotte, and her mouth was as crimson as if she'd been eating raspberries. She lay on satin sheets with a jewelled mask on her face and a hand between her legs, ecstatic, orgasmic, all I ever wanted: Charlotte.

She was appearing under the name of Titania, and was draped with peacock feathers. She worked, I was informed by the insectile black words that crept around her photographs, in an estate agent's in the South. She liked sensitive, honest men. She was nineteen.

And, goddamnit, she *looked* nineteen. And I was broke, on the dole with just over a million others, and going nowhere.

I sold my record collection, and my books, all but four copies of *Penthouse*, and most of the furniture, and I bought myself a fairly good camera. Then I phoned all the photographers I'd known when I was in advertising, almost a decade before.

Most of them didn't remember me, or they said they didn't. And those that did, didn't want an eager young assistant who wasn't young any more and had no experience. But I kept trying, and eventually got hold of Harry Bleak, a silver-haired old boy, with his own studios in Crouch End and a posse of expensive little boyfriends.

I told him what I wanted. He didn't even stop to think about it. "Be here in two hours."

"No catches?"

"Two hours. No more."

I was there.

For the first year I cleaned the studio, painted backdrops, and went out to the local shops and streets to beg, buy or borrow appropriate props. The next year he let me help with the lights, set up shots, waft smoke pellets and dry-ice around, and make the tea. I'm exaggerating — I only made the tea once; I make terrible tea. But I learned a hell of a lot about photography.

And suddenly it was 1981, and the world was newly romantic, and I was thirty-five and feeling every minute of it. Bleak told me to look after the studio for a few weeks, while he went off to Morocco for a month of well-earned debauchery.

She was in *Penthouse* that month. More coy and prim than before, waiting for me neatly between advertisements for stereos and scotch. She was called Dawn, but she was still my Charlotte, with nipples like beads of blood on her tanned breasts, dark, fuzzy thatch between forever legs, shot on location on a beach somewhere. She was only nineteen, said the text. Charlotte. Dawn.

Harry Bleak was killed travelling back from Morocco: a bus fell on him.

It's not funny, really — he was on a car-ferry coming back from Calais, and he snuck down into the car-hold to get his cigars, which he'd left in the glove compartment of the Merc.

The weather was rough, and a tourist bus (belonging, I read in the papers, and was told at length by a tearful boyfriend, to a shopping co-op in Wigan) hadn't been chained down properly. Harry was crushed against the side of his silver Mercedes.

He had always kept that car spotless.

When the will was read I discovered that the old bastard had left me his studio. I cried myself to sleep that night, got stinking drunk for a week, and then opened for business.

Things happened between then and now. I got married. It lasted three weeks, then we called it a day. I guess I'm not the marrying type. I got beaten up by a drunken Glaswegian on a train, late one night, and the other passengers pretended it wasn't happening. I bought a couple of terrapins and a tank, put them in the flat over the studio, and called them Rodney and Kevin. I became a fairly good photographer. I did calendars, advertising, fashion and glamour work, little kids and big stars: the works.

And, one spring day in 1985, I met Charlotte.

I was alone in the studio on a Thursday morning, unshaven and bare-foot. It was a free day, and I was going to spend it cleaning the place and reading the papers. I had left the studio doors open, letting the fresh air in to replace the stink of cigarettes and spilled wine of the shoot the night before, when a woman's voice said, "Bleak Photographic?"

"That's right," I said, not turning around, "but Bleak's dead. I run the place now."

"I want to model for you," she said.

I turned around. She was about five foot six, with honey-coloured hair, olive-green eyes, a smile like cold water in the desert.

"Charlotte?"

She tilted her head to one side. "If you like. Do you want to take my picture?"

I nodded dumbly. Plugged in the umbrellas, stood her up against a bare brick wall, and shot off a couple of test polaroids. No special makeup, no set, just a few lights, a Hasselblad, and the most beautiful girl in my world.

After a while she began to take off her clothes. I did not ask her to. I don't remember saying *anything* to her. She undressed and I carried on taking photographs.

She knew it all. How to pose, to preen, to stare. Silently she flirted with the camera, and with me standing behind it, moving around her, clicking

118

away. I don't remember stopping for anything, but I must have changed films, because I wound up with a dozen rolls at the end of the day.

I suppose you think that after the pictures were taken, I made love with her. Now, I'd be a liar if I said I've never screwed models in my time, and, for that matter, some of them have screwed me. But I didn't touch her. She was my dream; and if you touch a dream it vanishes, like a soap bubble.

And anyway, I simply couldn't touch her.

"How old are you?" I asked her just before she left, when she was pulling on her coat and picking up her bag.

"Nineteen," she told me without looking round, and then she was out the door.

She didn't say good-bye.

I sent the photos to *Penthouse*. I couldn't think of anywhere else to send them. Two days later I got a call from the Art Editor. "Loved the girl! Real face-of-the-Eighties stuff. What are her vital statistics?"

"Her name is Charlotte," I told him. "She's nineteen."

And now I'm thirty-nine, and one day I'll be fifty, and she'll still be nineteen. But someone else will be taking the photographs.

Rachel, my dancer, married an architect.

The blond punkette from Canada runs a multinational fashion chain. I do some photographic work for her from time to time. Her hair's cut short, and there's a smudge of grey in it, and she's a lesbian these days. She told me she's still got the mink sheets, but she made up the bit about the gold vibrator.

My ex-wife married a nice bloke who owns two video rental shops, and they moved to Slough. They have twin boys.

I don't know what happened to the maid.

And Charlotte?

In Greece, the philosophers are debating, Socrates is drinking hemlock, and she's posing for a sculpture of Erato, muse of light poetry and lovers, and she's nineteen.

In Crete she's oiling her breasts, and she's jumping bulls in the ring while King Minos applauds, and someone's painting her likeness on a wine-jar, and she's nineteen.

ANGELS AND VISITATIONS

In 2065 she's stretched out on the revolving floor of a holographic photographer, who records her as an erotic dream in Living Sensolove, imprisons the sight and sound and the very smell of her in a tiny diamond matrix. She's only nineteen.

And a caveman outlines Charlotte with a burnt stick on the wall of the temple cave, filling in the shape and texture of her with earths and berry-dyes. Nineteen.

Charlotte is there, in all places, all times, sliding through our fantasies, a girl forever.

I want her so much it makes me hurt sometimes. That's when I take down the photographs of her, and just look at them for a while, wondering why I didn't try to touch her, why I wouldn't really even speak to her when she was there, and never coming up with an answer that I could understand.

That's why I've written this all down, I suppose.

This morning I noticed yet another grey hair at my temple. Charlotte is nineteen. Somewhere.

Post-Mortem on Our Love

I've been dissecting all the letters that you sent me,
slicing through them looking for the real you
cutting through the fat and gristle of each tortuous epistle
trying to work out what to do.

I've laid the presents that you gave me out upon the floor
A book with pages missing, and a bottle, and a glove.
Now outside it's chilly autumn, I'm conducting a post-mortem
On our love.

I'm conducting a post-mortem on our love.
An autopsy to find out what went wrong.
I know it died.
I just don't know how, or why.
Maybe its heart stopped.

There's an eyeball in a bottle staring sadly at the morgue
There's a white line on the sidewalk silhouetting where it fell
In the dark I am inspecting all the angles of trajectory
Of Hell.

Was it suicide, or murder, or an accident, or what?
Though I cut and slice and saw and hack it won't come back to life
And I'm severing the label of each organ on the table
With a knife...

ANGELS AND VISITATIONS

I'm conducting a post-mortem on our love.
An autopsy to find out what went wrong.
I know it died.
I just don't know how, or why.
Maybe its heart stopped.

Being an Experiment
Upon Strictly Scientific Lines

Assisted by Unwins Ltd, Wine Merchants (Uckfield)

I**T STRUCK** me last night, after a couple of drinks, that I'd never heard of anyone experimentally testing the precise effects alcohol has on a creative writer.

I have in front of me a large bottle of scotch, a small bucket of ice, and a number of glasses. Also a typewriter, and some paper. All this in the spirit of purest scientific enquiry.

My plan is this: I will drink whilst writing. Thus, we will discover whether, for example, alcohol really does enhance one's creativity; or whether, as some have claimed (with, I suspect, scant evidence), it causes a writer to become maudlin, aggressive, rambling, and to lose his or her sense of modesty, decency and restraint.

Quiet, please. I am about to pour — and consume — my first drink.

(*Drink number one.*)

There.

Does booze make one more loquacious? Funnier? More intelligent? What is the relationship between alcohol and art? And what was it that poet said? You know, what's-his-name, rhymes with Heathcote Williams, made tents. Tip of my tongue. Omar Khayyam. "*I often wonder what the vintner buys, one-half so precious as the stuff he sells...*" Sheer poetry.

Excuse me.

(*Drink number two.*)

The word whisky, of course, comes from the Gaelic *uisge-a-bagh,* meaning water of life.

Angels and Visitations

I wonder how many great works of literature have been created due to alcohol.

I wonder how many great works of literature have been held up due to people having put their Tippex down and not being able to find it for ten minutes until eventually it turned up right in front of them all the time.

I wonder why my glass is empty. Excuse me.

(*Drink number three*)

Where was I? Oh yes. Alcohol. Writing.

I don't know *why* people say that drinking makes you aggressive. Writers are *not* an aggressive bunch. We're actually meek and mild and polite. Even when we've been drinking. *Especially* when we've been drinking.

I don't know what kind of numbskulled, guacamole-brained, gutless *wimps* would accuse writers of being aggressive. If *they* want to say that kind of stuff to me *I'll* be ready.

Drawn fucking typewriters at dawn.

Course *they'd* never show up. They got no bottle.

I got a bottle, which is oddly enough half-empty. And speaking as an impartial observer, the contents has haved no discernable effect on my writing whatsoever.

(*Drink number five.*)

Many writers such as for example myself have the TV on while working, because it is an educational instrument of great worth.

You can learn a lot from the television.

Omar Khayyam was on the other day, no, hold on, it was the other one, Heathcliff Williams, anyway he was on TV going on about big grey buggers, long noses, flappy ears, not hippos, the other ones, elephants, anyway, he was saying that the average ejaculate of an elephant would feed an ant-hill for a year.

Which is impressive I suppose, but I keep feeling sorry for the ants. Just think about it.

I mean, somewhere around March some little ant is going to say "Oh *no*. Not elephant spunk *again*!"

"Eat your ejaculate, dear. Furnished by pulsing elephant testicles, that was. Full of vitamins and protein."

"But we bin eatin it since January! I'm sick of it. Can't we go and chomp leaves, or milk one of those little sticky buggers, climb all over your roses, you know. Things. Wossnames. Aphids."

And the other one says, "I'll have you know there's ants in hills not far from here that'd be *very* grateful for nice plate of elephant come."

Poor little wossnames.

Ants.

I'll drink to them.

(*Drink number seven. Or jus' possibly drink six. Hang on. I'll count the empty glasses.*

Right. Drink five. Said it was drink five. Right.)

S'funny cos I have noticed along with many other great writers like Omar Williams and Heathcote Khayyam and people, how ones powers of inspiration start increasing practically exponentiallially under the influence.

Jus had this great idea fr a novel. No, s wunnerfl idea. Lissn. This bloke, right, some bloke, jus like this guy sort of bloke youd meet inna pub, good bloke always stans his roun, anyway, he meets this woman, an...

damlostit.

No, anyway, sagreat idea, cos he, um. Sjust like um Romeo an Thing, you know, exzcept he's in advertising, and she, I dunno, dyes her hair or somethng, dusn't mattr, anyWay... In the en they all live happily ever aftedr, sgonna b fuckig great you lissen, sellafuckin film rights anyday that calls for another drunk.

(*Drink numbers six seven qnd eight well finish the bottle atuqaly.*)

Whuwuz I?

Effec of drinkin on literry creativitity, thasswot.

Strrific.

Feel so bloody creative.

Feel absolutley cretive...

Actully feel a bit sick.

Escuse me.

Gotr escuse mysel.

Bak inaa minut.

o god.

We Can Get
Them For You Wholesale

Peter Pinter had never heard of Aristippus of the Cyrenaics, a lesser-known follower of Socrates, who maintained that the avoidance of trouble was the highest attainable good; however, he had lived his uneventful life according to this precept. In all respects except one (an inability to pass up a bargain, and which of us is entirely free from that?) he was a very moderate man. He did not go to extremes. His speech was proper and reserved; he rarely overate; he drank enough to be sociable and no more; he was far from rich, and in no wise poor. He liked people and people liked him. Bearing all that in mind, would you expect to find him in a lowlife pub on the seamier side of London's East End, taking out what is colloquially known as a "contract" on someone he hardly knew? You would not. You would not even expect to find him in the pub.

And until a certain Friday afternoon, you would have been right. But the love of a woman can do strange things to a man, even one so colourless as Peter Pinter, and the discovery that Miss Gwendolyn Thorpe, twenty-three years of age, of 9, Oaktree Terrace, Purley, was messing about (as the vulgar would put it) with a smooth young gentleman from the accounting department — *after*, mark you, she had consented to wear an engagement ring, composed of real ruby chips, nine-carat gold, and something that might well have been a diamond (£37.50) that it had taken Peter almost an entire lunch-hour to choose — can do very strange things to a man indeed.

After he made this shocking discovery Peter spent a sleepless Friday night, tossing and turning, with visions of Gwendolyn and Archie Gibbons (the Don Juan of Clamages Accounting Department) dancing and swimming before his eyes — performing acts that even Peter, if he were pressed, would have to admit were most improbable. But the bile of jealousy had risen up within him, and by the morning Peter had resolved that his rival should be done away with.

Saturday morning was spent wondering how one contacted an assassin, for, to the best of Peter's knowledge, none were employed by Clamages (the department store that employed all three of the members of our eternal triangle, and, incidentally, furnished the ring), and he was wary of asking anyone outright for fear of attracting attention to himself.

Thus it was that Saturday afternoon found him hunting through the Yellow Pages.

Assassins, he found, was not between *Asphalt Contractors* and *Assessors (Quantity)*; *Killers* was not between *Kennels* and *Kindergartens*; *Murderers* was not between *Mowers* and *Museums*. *Pest Control* looked promising; however closer investigation of the Pest Control advertisements showed them to be almost solely concerned with "rats, mice, fleas, cockroaches, rabbits, moles, and rats" (to quote from one that Peter felt was rather hard on rats), and not really what he had in mind. Even so, being of a careful nature, he dutifully inspected the entries in that category, and at the bottom of the second page, in small print, he found a firm that looked promising.

"Complete discreet disposal of irksome and unwanted mammals, etc." went the entry, *"Ketch, Hare, Burke and Ketch. The Old Firm."* It went on, to give no address, but only a telephone number.

Peter dialled the number, surprising himself by so doing. His heart pounded in his chest, and he tried to look nonchalant. The telephone rang once, twice, three times. Peter was just starting to hope that it would not be answered and he could forget the whole thing, when there was a click and a brisk young female voice said, "Ketch Hare Burke Ketch, can I help you?"

Carefully not giving his name Peter said, "Er, how big — I mean, what size mammals do you go up to? To, uh, dispose of?"

"Well, that would all depend on what size sir requires."

He plucked up all his courage. "A person?"

Her voice remained brisk and unruffled. "Of course, sir. Do you have a pen and paper handy? Good. Be at the Dirty Donkey pub, off Little Courtney Street, E3, tonight at eight o'clock. Carry a rolled-up copy of the *Financial*

Times — that's the pink one, sir — and our operative will approach you there." Then she put down the phone.

Peter was elated. It had been far easier than he had imagined. He went down to the newsagent's and bought a copy of the *Financial Times*, found Little Courtney Street in his *A-Z of London*, and spent the rest of the afternoon watching football on the television and imagining the smooth young gentleman from accounting's funeral.

It took Peter a while to find the pub. Eventually he spotted the pub sign, which showed a donkey, and was indeed remarkably dirty.

The Dirty Donkey was a small and more-or-less filthy pub, poorly lit, in which knots of unshaven people wearing dusty donkey jackets stood around eyeing each other suspiciously, eating crisps and drinking pints of Guinness, a drink that Peter had never cared for. Peter held his *Financial Times* under one arm, as conspicuously as he could, but no one approached him, so he bought a half of shandy and retreated to a corner table. Unable to think of anything else to do while waiting he tried to read the paper, but, lost and confused by a maze of grain futures, and a rubber company that was selling something or other short (quite what the short somethings were he could not tell), he gave it up and stared at the door.

He had waited almost ten minutes when a small, busy man hustled in, looked quickly around him, then came straight over to Peter's table and sat down.

He stuck out his hand. "Kemble. Burton Kemble, of Ketch Hare Burke Ketch. I hear you have a job for us."

He didn't look like a killer, Peter said so.

"Oh lor' bless us no. I'm not actually part of our workforce, sir. I'm in sales."

Peter nodded. That certainly made sense. "Can we — er — talk freely here?"

"Sure. Nobody's interested. Now then, how many people would you like disposed of?"

"Only one. His name's Archibald Gibbons and he works in Clamages accounting department. His address is..."

Kemble interrupted. "We can go into all that later, sir, if you don't mind. Let's just quickly go over the financial side. First of all, the contract will cost you £500..."

Peter nodded. He could afford that, and in fact had expected to have to pay a little more.

"...although there's always the special offer," Kemble concluded smoothly.

Peter's eyes shone. As I mentioned earlier, he loved a bargain, and often bought things he had no imaginable use for in sales or on special offers. Apart from this one failing (one that so many of us share), he was a most moderate young man. "Special offer?"

"Two for the price of one, sir."

Mmm. Peter thought about it. That worked out at only £250 each, which couldn't be bad no matter how you looked at it. There was only one snag. "I'm afraid I don't *have* anyone else I want killed."

Kemble looked disappointed. "That's a pity, sir. For two we could probably have even knocked the price down to, well, say £450 the both of them."

"Really?"

"Well, it gives our operatives something to do, sir. If you must know," and here he dropped his voice, "there really isn't enough work in this particular line to keep them occupied. Not like the old days. Isn't there just *one* other person you'd like to see dead?"

Peter pondered. He hated to pass up a bargain, but couldn't for the life of him think of anyone else. He liked people. Still, a bargain was a bargain...

"Look," said Peter. "Could I think about it, and see you here tomorrow night?"

The salesman looked pleased. "Of course, sir." he said. "I'm sure you'll be able to think of someone."

The answer — the obvious answer — came to Peter as he was drifting off to sleep that night. He sat straight up in bed, fumbled the bedside light on and wrote a name down on the back of an envelope, in case he forgot it. To tell the truth he didn't think that he could forget it, for it was painfully obvious, but you can never tell with these late-night thoughts.

The name that he had written down on the back of the envelope was this: Gwendolyn Thorpe.

He turned the light off, rolled over and was soon asleep, dreaming peaceful and remarkably un-murderous dreams.

Kemble was waiting for him when he arrived in the Dirty Donkey on Sunday night. Peter bought a drink and sat down beside him.

"I'm taking you up on the special offer," he said, by way of introduction.

Kemble nodded vigorously. "A very wise decision, if you don't mind me saying so, sir."

Peter Pinter smiled modestly, in the manner of one who read the *Financial Times* and made wise business decisions. "That will be £450, I believe?"

"Did I say £450, sir? Good gracious me, I do apologise. I beg your pardon, I was thinking of our bulk rate. It would be £475 for two people."

Disappointment mingled with cupidity on Peter's bland and youthful face. That was an extra twenty-five pounds. However, something that Kemble had said caught his attention.

"Bulk rate?"

"Of course, but I doubt that sir would be interested in that."

"No, no I am. Tell me about it."

"Very well, sir. Bulk rate, £450, would be for a large job. Ten people."

Peter wondered if he had heard correctly. "Ten people? But that's only £45 each."

"Yes, sir. It's the large order that makes it profitable."

"I see," said Peter, and "Hmm," said Peter and "Could you be here the same time tomorrow night?"

"Of course, sir."

Upon arriving home Peter got out a scrap of paper and a pen. He wrote the numbers one to ten down one side and then filled it in as follows:

1)...*Archie G.*

2)...*Gwennie.*

3)...

and so forth.

We Can Get Them For You Wholesale

Having filled in the first two he sat sucking his pen, hunting for wrongs done to him and people the world would be better off without.

He smoked a cigarette. He strolled around the room.

Aha! There was a physics teacher at a school he had attended who had delighted in making his life a misery. What was the man's name again? And for that matter, was he still alive? Peter wasn't sure, but he wrote *The Physics Teacher, Abbot Street Secondary School* next to the number three. The next came more easily — his department head had refused to raise his salary a couple of months back; that the raise had eventually come was immaterial. *Mr Hunterson* was number four.

When he was five a boy named Simon Ellis had poured paint on his head, while another boy named James somebody-or-other had held him down and a girl named Sharon Hartsharpe had laughed. They were numbers five through seven respectively.

Who else?

There was the man on television with the annoying snicker who read the news. He went down the list. And what about the woman in the flat next door, with the little yappy dog that shat in the hall? He put her and the dog down on nine. Ten was the hardest. He scratched his head and went into the kitchen for a cup of coffee, then dashed back and wrote *My Great Uncle Mervyn* down in the tenth place. The old man was rumoured to be quite affluent and there was a possibility (albeit rather slim) that he could leave Peter some money.

With the satisfaction of an evening's work well done he went off to bed.

Monday at Clamages was routine; Peter was a senior sales assistant in the books department, a job that actually entailed very little. He clutched his list tightly in his hand, deep in his pocket, rejoicing in the feeling of power that it gave him. He spent a most enjoyable lunch hour in the canteen with young Gwendolyn (who did not know that he had seen her and Archie enter the stockroom together), and even smiled at the smooth young man from the accounting department when he passed him in the corridor.

He proudly displayed his list to Kemble that evening.

The little salesman's face fell.

"I'm afraid this isn't ten people, Mr Pinter," he explained. "You've counted the woman in the next-door flat *and* her dog as one person. That brings it

131

to eleven, which would be an extra...." his pocket calculator was rapidly deployed, "...an extra seventy pounds. How about if we forget the dog?"

Peter shook his head. "The dog's as bad as the woman. Or worse."

"Then I'm afraid we have a slight problem. Unless..."

"What?"

"Unless you'd like to take advantage of our wholesale rate. But of course sir wouldn't be..."

There are words that do things to people; words that make people's faces flush with joy, excitement, or passion. *Environmental* can be one, *occult* is another. *Wholesale* was Peter's. He leaned back in his chair. "Tell me about it," he said, with the practised assurance of an experienced shopper.

"Well, sir," said Kemble, allowing himself a little chuckle, "We can, uh, *get* them for you, wholesale. £17.50 each, for every quarry after the first fifty, or a tenner each for every one over two hundred."

"I suppose you'd go down to a fiver if I wanted a thousand people knocked off?"

"Oh no, sir," Kemble looked shocked. "If you're talking those sorts of figures we can do them for a quid each."

"One *pound*?"

"That's right, sir. There's not a big profit margin on it, but the high turnover and productivity more than justifies it."

Kemble got up. "Same time tomorrow, sir?"

Peter nodded.

One thousand pounds. One thousand people. Peter Pinter didn't even *know* a thousand people. Even so...there were the Houses of Parliament. He didn't like politicians, they squabbled and argued and carried on so.

And for that matter...

An idea, shocking in its audacity. Bold. Daring. Still, the idea was there and it wouldn't go away. A distant cousin of his had married the younger brother of an earl or a baron or something...

On the way home from work that afternoon he stopped off at a little shop that he had passed a thousand times without entering. It had a large sign in the window — guaranteeing to trace your lineage for you, and even draw up a coat of arms if you happened to have mislaid your own — and an impressive heraldic map.

They were very helpful and phoned him up just after seven to give him their news.

If approximately fourteen million, seventy-two thousand, eight hundred and eleven people died, he, Peter Pinter, would be *King of England*.

He didn't have fourteen million, seventy-two thousand, eight hundred and eleven pounds: but he suspected that when you were talking in those figures, Mr Kemble would have one of his special discounts.

Mr Kemble did.

He didn't even raise an eyebrow.

"Actually," he explained, "it works out quite cheaply; you see we wouldn't have to do them all individually. Small-scale nuclear weapons, some judicious bombing, gassing, plague, dropping radios in swimming pools and then mopping up the stragglers. Say four thousand pounds."

"Four thou—? That's in*cred*ible!"

The salesman looked pleased with himself. "Our operatives will be glad of the work, sir." He grinned. "We pride ourselves on servicing our whole-sale customers."

The wind blew cold as Peter left the pub, setting the old sign swinging. It didn't look much like a dirty donkey, thought Peter; more like a pale horse.

Peter was drifting off to sleep that night, mentally rehearsing his Coronation Speech, when a thought drifted into his head and hung around. It would not go away. Could he — could he *possibly* be passing up an even larger saving than he already had? Could he be missing out on a bargain?

Peter climbed out of bed and walked over to the phone. It was almost three a.m., but even so...

His Yellow Pages lay open, where he had left it the previous Saturday, and he dialled the number.

The phone seemed to ring forever. There was a click and a bored voice said "Burke Hare Ketch, can I help you?"

"I hope I'm phoning too late..." he began.

"Of course not, sir."

"I was wondering if I could speak to Mr Kemble."

"Can you hold? I'll see if he's available."

Peter waited for a couple of minutes, listening to the ghostly crackles and whispers that always echo down empty phone lines.

"Are you there, caller?"

"Yes. I'm here."

"Putting you through." There was a buzz, then "Kemble speaking."

"Ah, Mr Kemble. Hello. Sorry if I got you out of bed or anything. This is, um, Peter Pinter."

"Yes, Mr Pinter?"

"Well, I'm sorry it's so late, only I was wondering...How much would it cost to kill everybody? Everybody in the world?"

"Everybody? All the people?"

"Yes. How much? I mean, for an order like that you'd have to have some kind of a big discount. How much would it be? For everyone?"

"Nothing at all, Mr Pinter."

"You mean you wouldn't do it?"

"I mean we'd do it for nothing, Mr Pinter. We only have to be asked, you see. We always have to be asked."

Peter was puzzled. "But — when would you start?"

"Start? Right away. Now. We've been ready for a long time. But we had to be asked, Mr Pinter. Goodnight. It *has* been a *pleasure* doing business with you."

The line went dead.

Peter felt strange. Everything seemed very distant. He wanted to sit down. What on earth had the man meant? *We always have to be asked.* It was definitely strange. Nobody does anything for nothing in this world; he had a good mind to phone Kemble back, and call the whole thing off. Perhaps he had overreacted; perhaps there was a perfectly innocent reason why Archie and Gwendolyn had entered the stock room together. He would talk to her; that's what he'd do. He'd talk to Gwennie first thing tomorrow morning...

That was when the noises started.

Odd cries from across the street. A cat fight? Foxes probably. He hoped someone would throw a shoe at them. Then, from the corridor outside his flat, he heard a muffled clumping, as if someone were dragging something very heavy along the floor. It stopped. Someone knocked on his door, twice, very softly.

Outside his window the cries were getting louder. Peter sat in his chair, knowing that somehow, somewhere, he had missed something. Something important. The knocking redoubled. He was thankful that he always locked and chained his door at night.

They'd been ready for a long time, but they had to be asked...

When the thing came through the door Peter started screaming, but he really didn't scream for very long.

THE MYSTERY OF
FATHER BROWN

AN ESSAY FROM *100 GREAT DETECTIVES*

IT IS not that the Father Brown stories lack colour. Chesterton was, after all, an artist, and begins almost every story by painting in light. "The evening daylight in the streets was large and luminous, opalescent and empty." ("The Man in the Passage"); "It was one of those chilly and empty afternoons in the early winter, when the daylight is silver rather than gold, and pewter rather than silver." ("The God of the Gongs"); "The sky was as Prussian a blue as Potsdam could require, but it was yet more like that lavish and glowing use of the colour which a child extracts from a shilling paint box."("The Fairy Tale of Father Brown") — three examples picked at random from *The Wisdom of Father Brown*, each occurring in the first paragraph.

We first meet him in "The Blue Cross", a bumbling Essex curate, laden down with brown paper parcels and an umbrella. Chesterton borrowed the parcels, the umbrella, and perhaps the central character from his friend Father John O'Connor — once he had discovered, with surprise, that a priest (whom society assumes to be unworldly) must by profession be on close terms with the World and its sins. "The Blue Cross" illustrates this principle: Flambeau, the master-thief, is out-thought every step of the way by the little priest, because the priest understands theft.

He had black clerical garb and a flat hat; sandy hair, and grey eyes as "empty as the North Sea". He was Father Brown (possible initial J, possible first name Paul), one of the greatest colourless figures of detective fiction, who continued through another sixty-odd short stories; less concerned with hounding down criminals, relentlessly bringing them to justice, or with solving crimes, than with offering the offender a chance at forgiveness, or merely being the commonsense vehicle that illuminates a Chestertonian paradox. Other great fictional detectives receive biographies, as aficionados backfill details of their lives and exploits (where *was* Watson's wound?); but Father Brown defies attempts to round out the details of his life outside of the canon. He had no home life, no early years, no last bow. He lacked colour.

It was Chesterton himself who pointed out that his subtitle to the novel *The Man Who Was Thursday*, "A Nightmare", tended to be overlooked. Perhaps that explains something else about the Father Brown stories: their logic is dream logic. The characters from a Father Brown story have little existence before the story starts, none after it has finished: each cast of inno-cents and malefactors is assembled to make the story work, and for no other reason. The tales are not exercises in deduction, for rarely is the reader pre-sented with a set of clues and logical problems to work through. Instead they are the inspired magic tricks of a master showman, or *tromp l'oeil* paintings in which the application of a little brown suddenly turns an Eastern swami into a private secretary, or a suicide into a murder and back again.

The Father Brown stories are a game of masks — it is rare that an unmasking of some kind does not occur. The denouement tends less to be a summation of misdirected clues, than a revelation of who, in the story one has read, was really whom.

It has been said that Chesterton was not proud of Father Brown; it is true that he wrote the stories, especially in the latter days, to fund *GK's Weekly*, the mouthpiece for his theories of Distributism (a sort of bucolic socialism, in which every right-thinking Englishman would own his own cow, and a plot of land to graze it on). It is also true that many of the Father Brown stories are repetitive; there are only so many masks, so many times a man can dis-guise himself as himself. But even the worst of the stories contains some-thing magical and rare: a sunset, perhaps, or a fabulous last line.

Chesterton himself was colourful, larger than life: one would imagine that in the creation of a detective he would have opted for the flamboyant — his hero would be a Flambeau, or a Sunday. Father Brown, on the other hand, seems created less as a detective than as a reaction to detectives, in a milieu in which, as GKC complained, "...the front of the cover shows somebody shot/ And the back of the cover will tell you the plot." ("Commercial Candour").

Angels and Visitations

You cannot celebrate Father Brown, for he doesn't exist. In the Chestertonian game of masks, the detective is the McGuffin, significant by his very insignificance. A plain little goblin of a man, less disorganised and flustered the more the tales go on, but still colourless to the extreme as he walks among the mirrors and the ever-changing lights.

"One of the wise and awful truths which this brown-paper art reveals is this," said Chesterton, discussing his fondness for drawing with chalks on brown paper, "that white is also a colour." And it is also a wise and awful truth that the most colourless of all detectives was employed to reveal the most colourful of all detective stories.

MURDER MYSTERIES

THIS IS true.

Ten years ago, give or take a year, I found myself on an enforced stopover in Los Angeles, a long way from home. It was December, and the California weather was warm and pleasant. England, however, was in the grip of fogs and snowstorms, and no planes were landing there. Each day I'd phone the airport, and each day I'd be told to wait another day.

This had gone on for almost a week.

I was barely out of my teens. Looking around today at the parts of my life left over from those days, I feel uncomfortable, as if I've received a gift, unasked, from another person: a house, a wife, children, a vocation. Nothing to do with me, I could say, innocently. If it's true that every seven years each cell in your body dies and is replaced, then I have truly inherited my life from a dead man; and the misdeeds of those times have been forgiven, and are buried with his bones.

I was in Los Angeles. Yes.

On the sixth day I received a message from an old sort-of-girlfriend from Seattle: she was in LA too, and she had heard I was around on the friends-of-friends network. Would I come over?

I left a message on her machine. Sure.

That evening: a small, blonde woman approached me, as I came out of the place I was staying. It was already dark.

She stared at me, as if she were trying to match me to a description, and then, hesitantly, she said my name.

"That's me. Are you Tink's friend?"

"Yeah. Car's out back. C'mon; she's really looking forward to seeing you."

The woman's car was one of the huge old boat-like jobs you only ever seem to see in California. It smelled of cracked and flaking leather upholstery. We drove out from wherever we were to wherever we were going.

Los Angeles was at that time a complete mystery to me; and I cannot say I understand it much better now. I understand London, and New York, and Paris: you can walk around them, get a sense of what's where in just a morning of wandering. Maybe catch the subway. But Los Angeles is about cars. Back then I didn't drive at all; even today I will not drive in America. Memories of LA for me are linked by rides in other people's cars, with no sense there of the shape of the city, of the relationships between the people and the place. The regularity of the roads, the repetition of structure and form, mean that when I try to remember it as an entity all I have is the boundless profusion of tiny lights I saw one night on my first trip to the city, from the hill of Griffith Park. It was one of the most beautiful things I had ever seen, from that distance.

"See that building?" said my blonde driver, Tink's friend. It was a red-brick art deco house, charming and quite ugly.

"Yes."

"Built in the 1930s," she said, with respect and pride.

I said something polite, trying to comprehend a city inside which fifty years could be considered a long time.

"Tink's real excited. When she heard you were in town. She was so excited."

"I'm looking forward to seeing her again."

Tink's real name was Tinkerbell Richmond. No lie.

She was staying with friends in small apartment clump, somewhere an hour's drive from downtown LA.

What you need to know about Tink: she was ten years older than me, in her early thirties; she had glossy black hair and red, puzzled lips, and very white skin, like Snow White in the fairy stories; the first time I met her I thought she was the most beautiful woman in the world.

Tink had been married for a while at some point in her life, and had a five-year-old daughter called Susan. I had never met Susan — when Tink had been in England, Susan had been staying on in Seattle, with her father.

People named Tinkerbell name their daughters Susan.

Memory is the great deceiver. Perhaps there are some individuals whose memories act like tape recordings, daily records of their lives complete in every detail, but I am not one of them. My memory is a patchwork of occurrences, of discontinuous events roughly sewn together: the parts I remember, I remember precisely, whilst other sections seem to have vanished completely.

I do not remember arriving at Tink's house, nor where her flatmate went.

What I remember next is sitting in Tink's lounge, with the lights low; the two of us next to each other, on the sofa.

We made small talk. It had been perhaps a year since we had seen one another. But a twenty-one-year-old boy has little to say to a thirty-two-year-old woman, and soon, having nothing in common, I pulled her to me.

She snuggled close with a kind of sigh, and presented her lips to be kissed. In the half-light her lips were black. We kissed for a little, and I stroked her breasts through her blouse, on the couch; and then she said:

"We can't fuck. I'm on my period."

"Fine."

"I can give you a blow job, if you'd like."

I nodded assent, and she unzipped my jeans, and lowered her head to my lap.

After I had come, she got up and ran into the kitchen. I heard her spitting into the sink, and the sound of running water: I remember wondering why she did it, if she hated the taste that much.

Then she returned and we sat next to each other on the couch.

"Susan's upstairs, asleep," said Tink. "She's all I live for. Would you like to see her?"

"I don't mind."

We went upstairs. Tink led me into a darkened bedroom. There were child-scrawl pictures all over the walls — wax-crayoned drawings of winged fairies and little palaces — and a small, fair-haired girl was asleep in the bed.

"She's very beautiful," said Tink, and kissed me. Her lips were still slightly sticky. "She takes after her father."

We went downstairs. We had nothing else to say, nothing else to do. Tink turned on the main light. For the first time I noticed tiny crows' feet at the corners of her eyes, incongruous on her perfect, Barbie-doll face.

"I love you," she said.

"Thank you."

"Would you like a ride back?"

"If you don't mind leaving Susan alone...?"

She shrugged, and I pulled her to me for the last time.

At night, Los Angeles is all lights. And shadows.

A blank, here, in my mind. I simply don't remember what happened next. She must have driven me back to the place where I was staying — how else would I have gotten there? I do not even remember kissing her good-bye. Perhaps I simply waited on the sidewalk and watched her drive away.

Perhaps.

I do know, however, that once I reached the place I was staying I just stood there, unable to go inside, to wash and then to sleep, unwilling to do anything else.

I was not hungry. I did not want alcohol. I did not want to read, or talk. I was scared of walking too far, in case I became lost, bedeviled by the repeating motifs of Los Angeles, spun around and sucked in so I could never find my way home again. Central Los Angeles sometimes seems to me to be nothing more than a pattern, like a set of repeating blocks: a gas station, a few homes, a mini-mall (donuts, photo developers, laundromats, fast-foods), and repeat until hypnotised; and the tiny changes in the mini-malls and the houses only serve to reinforce the structure.

I thought of Tink's lips. Then I fumbled in a pocket of my jacket, and pulled out a packet of cigarettes.

I lit one, inhaled, blew blue smoke into the warm night air.

There was a stunted palm tree growing outside the place I was staying, and I resolved to walk for a way, keeping the tree in sight, to smoke my cigarette, perhaps even to think; but I felt too drained to think. I felt very sexless, and very alone.

A block or so down the road there was a bench, and when I reached it I sat down. I threw the stub of the cigarette onto the pavement, hard, and watched it shower orange sparks.

Someone said, "I'll buy a cigarette off you, pal. Here."

A hand, in front of my face, holding a quarter. I looked up.

He did not look old, although I would not have been prepared to say how old he was. Late thirties, perhaps. Mid-forties. He wore a long, shabby coat, colorless under the yellow street lamps, and his eyes were dark.

"Here. A quarter. That's a good price."

I shook my head, pulled out the packet of Marlboros, offered him one. "Keep your money. It's free. Have it."

He took the cigarette. I passed him a book of matches (it advertised a telephone sex line; I remember that), and he lit the cigarette. He offered me the matches back, and I shook my head. "Keep them. I always wind up accumulating books of matches in America."

"Uh-huh." He sat next to me, and smoked his cigarette. When he had smoked it halfway down, he tapped the lighted end off on the concrete, stubbed out the glow, and placed the butt of the cigarette behind his ear.

"I don't smoke much," he said. "Seems a pity to waste it, though."

A car careened down the road, veering from one side to the other. There were four young men in the car: the two in the front were both pulling at the wheel, and laughing. The windows were wound down, and I could hear their laughter, and the two in the back seat (*"Gaary, you asshole! What the fuck are you onnn mannnn?"*) and the pulsing beat of a rock song. Not a song I recognised. The car looped around a corner, out of sight.

Soon the sounds were gone, too.

"I owe you," said the man on the bench.

"Sorry?"

"I owe you something. For the cigarette. And the matches. You wouldn't take the money. I owe you."

I shrugged, embarrassed. "Really, it's just a cigarette. I figure, if I give people cigarettes, then if ever I'm out, maybe people will give me cigarettes."

I laughed, to show I didn't really mean it, although I did. "Don't worry about it."

"Mm. You want to hear a story? True story? Stories always used to be good payment. These days..." He shrugged. "... Not so much."

I sat back on the bench, and the night was warm, and I looked at my watch: it was almost one in the morning. In England a freezing new day would already have begun: a workday would be starting for those who could beat the snow and get into work; another handful of old people, and those without homes, would have died, in the night, from the cold.

"Sure," I said to the man. "Sure. Tell me a story."

He coughed, grinned white teeth — a flash in the darkness — and he began.

"First thing I remember was the Word. And the Word was God. Sometimes, when I get *really* down, I remember the sound of the Word in my head, shaping me, forming me, giving me life.

"The Word gave me a body, gave me eyes. And I opened my eyes, and I saw the light of the Silver City.

"I was in a room — a silver room — and there wasn't anything in it except me. In front of me was a window, that went from floor to ceiling, open to the sky, and through the window I could see the spires of the City, and at the edge of the City, the Dark.

"I don't know how long I waited there. I wasn't impatient or anything, though. I remember that. It was like I was waiting until I was called; and I knew that some time I would be called. And if I had to wait until the end of everything, and never be called, why, that was fine too. But I'd be called, I was certain of that. And then I'd know my name, and my function.

"Through the window I could see silver spires, and in many of the other spires were windows; and in the windows I could see others like me. That was how I knew what I looked like.

"You wouldn't think it of me, seeing me now, but I was beautiful. I've come down in the world a way since then.

"I was taller then, and I had wings.

"They were huge and powerful wings, with feathers the colour of mother-of-pearl. They came out from just between my shoulderblades. They were so good. My wings.

144

"Sometimes I'd see others like me, the ones who'd left their rooms, who were already fulfilling their duties. I'd watch them soar through the sky from spire to spire, performing errands I could barely imagine.

"The sky above the City was a wonderful thing. It was always light, although lit by no sun — lit, perhaps by the City itself: but the quality of light was forever changing. Now pewter-coloured light, then brass, then a gentle gold, or a soft and quiet amethyst..."

The man stopped talking. He looked at me, his head on one side. There was a glitter in his eyes that scared me. "You know what amethyst is? A kind of purple stone?"

I nodded.

My crotch felt uncomfortable.

It occurred to me then that the man might not be mad; I found this far more disquieting than the alternative.

The man began talking once more. "I don't know how long it was that I waited, in my room. But time didn't mean anything. Not back then. We had all the time in the world.

"The next thing that happened to me, was when the Angel Lucifer came to my cell. He was taller than me, and his wings were imposing, his plumage perfect. He had skin the colour of sea-mist, and curly silver hair, and these wonderful grey eyes...

"I say *he*, but you should understand that none of us had any sex, to speak of." He gestured towards his lap. "Smooth and empty. Nothing there. You know.

"Lucifer shone. I mean it — he glowed from inside. All angels do. They're lit up from within, and in my cell the angel Lucifer burned like a lightning storm.

"He looked at me. And he named me.

"'You are Raguel,' he said. 'The Vengeance of the Lord.'

"I bowed my head, because I knew it was true. That was my name. That was my function.

"'There has been a...a wrong thing,' he said. 'The first of its kind. You are needed.'

"He turned and pushed himself into space, and I followed him, flew behind him across the Silver City, to the outskirts, where the City stops and the Darkness begins; and it was there, under a vast silver spire, that we descended to the street, and I saw the dead angel.

"The body lay, crumpled and broken, on the silver sidewalk. Its wings were crushed underneath it and a few loose feathers had already blown into the silver gutter.

"The body was almost dark. Now and again a light would flash inside it, an occasional flicker of cold fire in the chest, or in the eyes, or in the sexless groin, as the last of the glow of life left it for ever.

"Blood pooled in rubies on its chest and stained its white wing-feathers crimson. It was very beautiful, even in death.

"It would have broken your heart.

"Lucifer spoke to me, then. 'You must find who was responsible for this, and how; and take the Vengeance of the Name on whosoever caused this thing to happen.'

"He really didn't have to say anything. I knew that already. The hunt, and the retribution: it was what I was created for, in the Beginning; it was what I *was*.

"'I have work to attend to,' said the angel Lucifer.

"He flapped his wings, once, hard, and rose upwards; the gust of wind sent the dead angel's loose feathers blowing across the street.

"I leaned down to examine the body. All luminescence had by now left it. It was a dark thing; a parody of an angel. It had a perfect, sexless face, framed by silver hair. One of the eyelids was open, revealing a placid grey eye; the other was closed. There were no nipples on the chest and only smoothness between the legs.

"I lifted the body up.

"The back of the angel was a mess. The wings were broken and twisted; the back of the head staved in; there was a floppiness to the corpse that made me think its spine had been broken as well. The back of the angel was all blood.

"The only blood on its front was in the chest area. I probed it with my forefinger, and it entered the body without difficulty.

"*He fell*, I thought. *And he was dead before he fell.*

"And I looked up at the windows that ranked the street. I stared across the Silver City. *You did this*, I thought. *I will find you, whoever you are. And I will take the Lord's vengeance upon you.*"

146

Angels and Visitations

The man took the cigarette stub from behind his ear, lit it with a match. Briefly I smelled the ashtray smell of a dead cigarette, acrid and harsh; then he pulled down to the unburnt tobacco, exhaled blue smoke into the night air.

"The angel who had first discovered the body was called Phanuel.

"I spoke to him in the Hall of Being. That was the spire beside which the dead angel lay. In the Hall hung the...the blueprints, maybe, for what was going to be...all this." He gestured with the hand that held the stubby cigarette, pointing to the night sky and the parked cars and the world. "You know. The universe."

"Phanuel was the senior designer; working under him were a multitude of angels labouring on the details of the Creation. I watched him from the floor of the hall. He hung in the air below the Plan, and angels flew down to him, waiting politely in turn as they asked him questions, checked things with him, invited comment on their work. Eventually he left them, and descended to the floor.

"'You are Raguel,' he said. His voice was high, and fussy. 'What need have you of me?'

"'You found the body?'

"'Poor Carasel? Indeed I did. I was leaving the hall — there are a number of concepts we are currently constructing, and I wished to ponder one of them, — *Regret* by name. I was planning to get a little distance from the City — to fly above it, I mean, not to go into the Dark outside, I wouldn't do that, although there has been a some loose talk amongst...but, yes. I was going to rise, and contemplate.

"'I left the Hall, and...,' he broke off. He was small, for an angel. His light was muted, but his eyes were vivid and bright. I mean really bright. 'Poor Carasel. How could he do that to himself? How?'

"'You think his destruction was self-inflicted?'

"He seemed puzzled — surprised that there could be any other explanation. 'But of course. Carasel was working under me, developing a number of concepts that shall be intrinsic to the Universe, when its Name shall be spoken. His group did a remarkable job on some of the real basics — *Dimension* was one, and *Sleep* another. There were others.

"'Wonderful work. Some of his suggestions regarding the use of individual viewpoints to define dimensions were truly ingenious.

"'Anyway. He had begun work on a new project. It's one of the really major ones — the ones that I would usually handle, or possibly even Zephkiel.' He glanced upward. 'But Carasel had done such sterling work. And his last project was so remarkable. Something apparently quite trivial, that he and Saraquael elevated into...' He shrugged. 'But that is unimportant. It was *this* project that forced him into non-being. But none of us could ever have foreseen...'

"'What was his current project?'

"Phanuel stared at me. 'I'm not sure I ought to tell you. All the new concepts are considered sensitive, until we get them into the final form in which they will be Spoken.'

"I felt myself transforming. I am not sure how I can explain it to you, but suddenly I wasn't me — I was something larger. I was transfigured: I was my function.

"Phanuel was unable to meet my gaze.

"'I am Raguel, who is the Vengeance of the Lord,' I told him. 'I serve the Name directly. It is my mission to discover the nature of this deed, and to take the Name's vengeance on those responsible. My questions are to be answered.'

"The little angel trembled, and he spoke fast.

"'Carasel and his partner were researching *Death*. Cessation of life. An end to physical, animated existence. They were putting it all together. But Carasel always went too far into his work — we had a terrible time with him when he was designing *Agitation*. That was when he was working on *Emotions...*'

"'You think Carasel died to — to research the phenomenon?'

"'Or because it intrigued him. Or because he followed his research just too far. Yes.' Phanuel flexed his fingers, stared at me with those brightly shining eyes. 'I trust that you will repeat none of this to any unauthorised persons, Raguel.'

"'What did you do when you found the body?'

"'I came out of the Hall, as I said, and there was Carasel on the sidewalk, staring up. I asked him what he was doing and he did not reply. Then I noticed the inner fluid, and that Carasel seemed unable, rather than unwilling, to talk to me.

"'I was scared. I did not know what to do.

"'The Angel Lucifer came up behind me. He asked me if there was some kind of problem. I told him. I showed him the body. And then...then his Aspect came upon him, and he communed with the Name. He burned so bright.

"'Then he said he had to fetch the one whose function embraced events like this, and he left — to seek you, I imagine.

"'As Carasel's death was now being dealt with, and his fate was no real concern of mine, I returned to work, having gained a new — and I suspect, quite valuable — perspective on the mechanics of *Regret*.

"'I am considering taking *Death* away from the Carasel and Saraquael partnership. I may reassign it to Zephkiel, my senior partner, if he is willing to take it on. He excels on contemplative projects.'

"By now there was a line of angels waiting to talk to Phanuel. I felt I had almost all I was going to get from him.

"'Who did Carasel work with? Who would have been the last to see him alive?'

"'You could talk to Saraquael, I suppose — he was his partner, after all. Now, if you'll excuse me...'

"He returned to his swarm of aides: advising, correcting, suggesting, forbidding."

The man paused.

The street was quiet, now; I remember the low whisper of his voice, the buzz of a cricket somewhere. A small animal — a cat perhaps, or something more exotic, a raccoon, or even a jackal — darted from shadow to shadow among the parked cars on the opposite side of the street.

"Saraquael was in the highest of the mezzanine galleries that ringed the Hall of Being. As I said, the Universe was in the middle of the Hall, and it glinted and sparkled and shone. Went up quite a way, too..."

"The Universe you mention, it was, what, a diagram?" I asked, interrupting for the first time.

"Not really. Kind of. Sorta. It was a blueprint; but it was full-sized, and it hung in the Hall, and all these angels went around and fiddled with it all the time. Doing stuff with *Gravity*, and *Music* and *Klar* and whatever. It wasn't really the universe, not yet. It would be, when it was finished, and it was time for it to be properly Named."

"But..." I grasped for words to express my confusion. The man interrupted me.

"Don't worry about it. Think of it as a model, if that makes it easier for you. Or a map. Or a — what's the word? Prototype. Yeah. A Model-T Ford universe." He grinned. "You got to understand, a lot of the stuff I'm telling you, I'm translating already; putting it in a form you can understand. Otherwise I couldn't tell the story at all. You want to hear it?"

"Yes." I didn't care if it was true or not; it was a story I needed to hear all the way through to the end.

"Good. So shut up and listen.

"So I met Saraquael, in the topmost gallery. There was no one else about — just him, and some papers, and some small, glowing models.

"'I've come about Carasel,' I told him.

"He looked at me. 'Carasel isn't here at this time,' he said. 'I expect him to return shortly.'

"I shook my head.

"'Carasel won't be coming back. He's stopped existing as a spiritual entity,' I said.

"His light paled, and his eyes opened very wide. 'He's dead?'

"'That's what I said. Do you have any ideas about how it happened?'

"'I...this is so sudden. I mean, he'd been talking about...but I had no idea that he would...'

"'Take it slowly.'

"Saraquael nodded.

"He stood up and walked to the window. There was no view of the Silver City from his window — just a reflected glow from the City and the sky behind us, hanging in the air, and beyond that, the Dark. The wind from the Dark gently caressed Saraquael's hair as he spoke. I stared at his back.

"'Carasel is...no, was. That's right, isn't it? *Was*. He was always so involved. And so creative. But it was never enough for him. He always wanted to understand everything — to experience what he was working on. He was never content to just create it — to understand it intellectually. He wanted *all* of it.

"'That wasn't a problem before, when we were working on properties of matter. But when we began to design some of the Named emotions...he got too involved with his work.

"'And our latest project was *Death*. It's one of the hard ones — one of the big ones, too, I suspect. Possibly it may even become the attribute that's going to define the Creation for the Created: if not for *Death*, they'd be content to simply exist, but with *Death*, well, their lives will have meaning — a boundary beyond which the living cannot cross...'

"'So you think he killed himself?'

"'I know he did,' said Saraquael. I walked to the window, and looked out. Far below, a *long* way, I could see a tiny white dot. That was Carasel's body. I'd have to arrange for someone to take care of it. I wondered what we would do with it; but there would be someone who would know, whose function was the removal of unwanted things. It was not my function. I knew that.

"'How?'

"He shrugged. 'I know. Recently he'd begun asking questions — questions about *Death*. How we could know whether or not it was right to make this thing, to set the rules, if we were not going to experience it ourselves. He kept talking about it.'

"'Didn't you wonder about this?'

"Saraquael turned, for the first time, to look at me. 'No. That *is* our function — to discuss, to improvise, to aid the Creation and the Created. We sort it out now, so that when it all Begins, it'll run like clockwork. Right now we're working on *Death*. So obviously that's what we look at. The physical aspect; the emotional aspect; the philosophical aspect...

"'And the *patterns*. Carasel had the notion that what we do here in the Hall of Being creates patterns. That there are structures and shapes appropriate to beings and events that, once begun, must continue until they reach their end. For us, perhaps, as well as for them. Conceivably he felt this was one of his patterns.'

"'Did you know Carasel well?'

"'As well as any of us know each other. We saw each other here; we worked side by side. At certain times I would retire to my cell, across the city. Sometimes he would do the same.'

"'Tell me about Phanuel.'

"His mouth crooked into a smile. 'He's officious. Doesn't do much — farms everything out, and takes all the credit.' He lowered his voice, although there was no other soul in the gallery. 'To hear him talk, you'd think that *Love* was all his own work. But to his credit, he does make sure the work gets done. Zephkiel's the real thinker of the two senior designers, but he doesn't come here. He stays back in his cell in the City, and contemplates; resolves problems from a distance. If you need to speak to Zephkiel, you go to Phanuel, and Phanuel relays your questions to Zephkiel...'

"I cut him short. 'How about Lucifer? Tell me about him.'

"'Lucifer? The Captain of the Host? He doesn't work here...He has visited the Hall a couple of times, though — inspecting the Creation. They say he reports directly to the Name. I have never spoken to him.'

"'Did he know Carasel?'

"'I doubt it. As I said, he has only been here twice. I have seen him on other occasions, though. Through here.' He flicked a wingtip, indicating the world outside the window. 'In flight.'

"'Where to?'

"Saraquael seemed to be about to say something; then he changed his mind. 'I don't know.'

"I looked out of the window, at the Darkness outside the Silver City.

"'I may want to talk with you some more, later,' I told Saraquael.

"'Very good.' I turned to go.

"'Sir? Do you know if they will be assigning me another partner? For *Death*?'

"'No,' I told him. 'I'm afraid I don't.'

"In the centre of the Silver City was a park — a place of recreation and rest. I found the Angel Lucifer there, beside a river. He was just standing, watching the water flow.

"'Lucifer?'

"He inclined his head. 'Raguel. Are you making progress?'

"'I don't know. Maybe. I need to ask you a few questions. Do you mind?'

"'Not at all.'

"'How did you come upon the body?'

"'I didn't. Not exactly. I saw Phanuel, standing in the street. He looked distressed. I enquired whether there was something wrong, and he showed me the dead angel. And I fetched you.'

"'I see.'

"He leaned down, let one hand enter the cold water of the river. The water splashed and rilled around it. 'Is that all?'

"'Not quite. What were you doing in that part of the City?'

"'I don't see what business that is of yours.'

"'It is my business, Lucifer. What were you doing there?'

"'I was...walking. I do that sometimes. Just walk, and think. And try to understand.' He shrugged.

"'You walk on the edge of the City?'

"A beat, then, 'Yes.'

"'That's all I want to know. For now.'

"'Who else have you talked to?'

"'Carasel's boss, and his partner. They both feel that he killed himself — ended his own life.'

"'Who else are you going to talk to?'

"I looked up. The spires of the City of the Angels towered above us. 'Maybe everyone.'

"'All of them?'

"'If I need to. It's my function. I cannot rest until I understand what happened, and until the vengeance of the Name has been taken on whosoever was responsible. But I'll tell you something I do know.'

"'What would that be?' Drops of water fell like diamonds from the angel Lucifer's perfect fingers.

"'Carasel did not kill himself.'

"'How do you know that?'

"'I am Vengeance. If Carasel had died by his own hand,' I explained to the Captain of the Heavenly Host, 'there would have been no call for me. Would there?'

"He did not reply.

"I flew upwards, into the light of the eternal morning.

"You got another cigarette on you?"

I fumbled out the red and white packet, handed him a cigarette.

"Obliged.

"Zephkiel's cell was larger than mine.

"It wasn't a place for waiting. It was a place to live, and work, and *be*. It was lined with books, and scrolls, and papers, and there were images and representations on the walls: pictures. I'd never seen a picture before.

"In the centre of the room was a large chair, and Zephkiel sat there, his eyes closed, his head back.

"As I approached him he opened his eyes.

"They burned no brighter than the eyes of any of the other angels I had seen, but somehow, they seemed to have seen more. It was something about the way he looked. I'm not sure I can explain it. And he had no wings.

"'Welcome, Raguel,' he said. He sounded tired.

"'You are Zephkiel?' I don't know why I asked him that. I mean, I knew who people were. It's part of my function, I guess. Recognition. I know who *you* are.

"'Indeed. You are staring, Raguel. I have no wings, it is true, but then, my function does not call for me to leave this cell. I remain here, and I ponder. Phanuel reports back to me, brings me the new things, for my opinion. He brings me the problems, and I think about them, and occasionally I make myself useful by making some small suggestions. That is my function. As yours is vengeance.'

"'Yes.'

"'You are here about the death of the angel Carasel?'

"'Yes.'

"'I did not kill him.'

"When he said it, I knew it was true.

"'Do you know who did?'

"'That is *your* function, is it not? To discover who killed the poor thing, and to take the Vengeance of the Name upon him.'

"'Yes.'

"He nodded.

"'What do you want to know?'

"I paused, reflecting on what I had heard that day. 'Do you know what Lucifer was doing in that part of the City, before the body was found?'

"The old angel stared at me. 'I can hazard a guess.'

"'Yes?'

"'He was walking in the Dark.'

"I nodded. I had a shape in my mind, now. Something I could almost grasp. I asked the last question:

"'What can you tell me about *Love*?'

"And he told me. And I thought I had it all.

"I returned to the place where Carasel's body had been. The remains had been removed, the blood had been cleaned away, the stray feathers collected and disposed of. There was nothing on the silver sidewalk to indicate it had ever been there. But I knew where it had been.

"I ascended on my wings, flew upward until I neared the top of the spire of the Hall of Being. There was a window there, and I entered.

"Saraquael was working there, putting a wingless mannikin into a small box. On one side of the box was a representation of a small brown creature, with eight legs. On the other was a representation of a white blossom.

"'Saraquael?'

"'Hm? Oh, it's you. Hello. Look at this: if you were to die, and to be, let us say, put into the earth in a box, which would you want laid on top of you — a spider, here, or a lily, here?'

"'The lily, I suppose.'

"'Yes, that's what I think, too. But why? I wish...'" He raised a hand to his chin, stared down at the two models, put first one on top of the box then the other, experimentally. 'There's so much to do, Raguel. So much to get right. And we only get one chance at it, you know. There'll just be one universe — we can't keep trying until we get it right. I wish I understood why all this was so important to Him...'

"'Do you know where Zephkiel's cell is?' I asked him.

"'Yes. I mean, I've never been there. But I know where it is.'

"'Good. Go there. He'll be expecting you. I will meet you there.'

"He shook his head. 'I have work to do. I can't just...'

"I felt my function come upon me. I looked down at him, and I said, 'You will be there. Go now.'

"He said nothing. He backed away from me, toward the window, staring at me; then he turned, and flapped his wings, and I was alone.

"I walked to the central well of the Hall, and let myself fall, tumbling down through the model of the universe: it glittered around me, unfamiliar colours and shapes seething and writhing without meaning.

"As I approached the bottom, I beat my wings, slowing my descent, and stepped lightly onto the silver floor. Phanuel stood between two angels, who were both trying to claim his attention.

"'I don't care how aesthetically pleasing it would be,' he was explaining to one of them. 'We simply cannot put it in the centre. Background radiation would prevent any possible life-forms from even getting a foothold; and anyway, it's too unstable.'

"He turned to the other. 'Okay, let's see it. Hmm. So that's *Green*, is it? It's not exactly how I'd imagined it, but. Mm. Leave it with me. I'll get back to you.' He took a paper from the angel, folded it over decisively.

"He turned to me. His manner was brusque, and dismissive. 'Yes?'

"'I need to talk to you.'

"'Mm? Well, make it quick. I have much to do. If this is about Carasel's death, I have told you all I know.'

"'It is about Carasel's death. But I will not speak to you now. Not here. Go to Zephkiel's cell: he is expecting you. I will meet you there.'

"He seemed about to say something, but he only nodded, walked toward the door.

"I turned to go, when something occurred to me. I stopped the angel who had the *Green*. 'Tell me something.'

"'If I can, sir.'

"'That thing.' I pointed to the Universe. 'What's it going to be *for*?'

"'For? Why, it is the Universe.'

"'I know what it's called. But what purpose will it serve?'

"He frowned. 'It is part of the plan. The Name wishes it; He requires *such and such*, to these dimensions, and having *such and such* properties and ingredients. It is our function to bring it into existence, according to His wishes. I am sure He knows its function, but He has not revealed it to me.' His tone was one of gentle rebuke.

"I nodded, and left that place.

"High above the City a phalanx of angels wheeled and circled and dove. Each held a flaming sword which trailed a streak of burning brightness behind it, dazzling the eye. They moved in unison through the salmon-pink sky. They were very beautiful. It was — you know on summer evenings, when you get whole flocks of birds performing their dances in the sky? Weaving and circling and clustering and breaking apart again, so just as you think you understand the pattern, you realise you don't, and you never will? It was like that, only better.

"Above me was the sky. Below me, the shining City. My home. And outside the City, the Dark.

"Lucifer hovered a little below the Host, watching their maneuvers.

"'Lucifer?'

"'Yes, Raguel? Have you discovered your malefactor?'

"'I think so. Will you accompany me to Zephkiel's cell? There are others waiting for us there, and I will explain everything.'

"He paused. Then, 'Certainly.'

"He raised his perfect face to the angels, now performing a slow revolution in the sky, each moving through the air keeping perfect pace with the next, none of them ever touching. 'Azazel!'

"An angel broke from the circle; the others adjusted almost imperceptibly to his disappearance, filling the space, so you could no longer see where he had been.

"'I have to leave. You are in command, Azazel. Keep them drilling. They still have much to perfect.'

"'Yes, sir.'

"Azazel hovered where Lucifer had been, staring up at the flock of angels, and Lucifer and I descended toward the city.

"'He's my second-in-command,' said Lucifer. 'Bright. Enthusiastic. Azazel would follow you anywhere.'

"'What are you training them for?'

"'War.'

"'With whom?'

"'How do you mean?'

"'Who are they going to fight? Who else *is* there?'

"He looked at me; his eyes were clear, and honest. 'I do not know. But He has Named us to be His army. So we will be perfect. For Him. The Name is infallible and all-just, and all-wise, Raguel. It cannot be otherwise, no matter what —' He broke off, and looked away.

"'You were going to say?'

"'It is of no importance.'

"'Ah.'

"We did not talk for the rest of the descent to Zephkiel's cell."

I looked at my watch: it was almost three. A chill breeze had begun to blow down the LA street, and I shivered. The man noticed, and he paused in his story. "You okay?" he asked.

"I'm fine. Please carry on. I'm fascinated."

He nodded.

"They were waiting for us in Zephkiel's cell: Phanuel, Saraquael, and Zephkiel. Zephkiel was sitting in his chair. Lucifer took up a position beside the window.

"I walked to centre of the room, and I began.

158

"'I thank you all for coming here. You know who I am; you know my function. I am the Vengeance of the Name: the arm of the Lord. I am Raguel.

"'The angel Carasel is dead. It was given to me to find out why he died, who killed him. This I have done. Now, the angel Carasel was a designer in the Hall of Being. He was very good, or so I am told...

"'Lucifer. Tell me what you were doing, before you came upon Phanuel, and the body.'

"'I have told you already. I was walking.'

"'Where were you walking?'

"'I do not see what business that is of yours.'

"'*Tell me.*'

"He paused. He was taller than any of us; tall, and proud. 'Very well. I was walking in the Dark. I have been walking in the Darkness for some time now. It helps me to gain a perspective on the City — being outside it. I see how fair it is, how perfect. There is nothing more enchanting than our home. Nothing more complete. Nowhere else that anyone would want to be.'

"'And what do you do in the Dark, Lucifer?'

"He stared at me. 'I walk. And....there are voices, in the Dark. I listen to the voices. They promise me things, ask me questions, whisper and plead. And I ignore them. I steel myself and I gaze at the City. It is the only way I have of testing myself — putting myself to any kind of trial. I am the Captain of the Host; I am the first among the Angels, and I must prove myself.'

"I nodded. 'Why did you not tell me this before?'

"He looked down. 'Because I am the only angel who walks in the Dark. Because I do not want others to walk in the Dark: I am strong enough to challenge the voices, to test myself. Others are not so strong. Others might stumble, or fall.'

"'Thank you, Lucifer. That is all, for now.' I turned to the next angel. 'Phanuel. How long have you been taking credit for Carasel's work?'

"His mouth opened, but no sound came out.

"'*Well?*'

"'I...I would not take credit for another's work.'

"'But you did take credit for *Love*?'

"He blinked. 'Yes. I did.'

"'Would you care to explain to us all what *Love* is?' I asked.

"He glanced around uncomfortably. 'It's a feeling of deep affection and attraction for another being, often combined with passion or desire — a need to be with another.' He spoke dryly, didactically, as if he were reciting a mathematical formula. 'The feeling that we have for the Name, for our Creator — that is *Love*...amongst other things. *Love* will be an impulse which will inspire and ruin in equal measure. We are...' He paused, then began once more. 'We are very proud of it.'

"He was mouthing the words. He no longer seemed to hold any hope that we would believe them.

"'Who did the majority of the work on *Love*? No, don't answer. Let me ask the others first. Zephkiel? When Phanuel passed the details on *Love* to you for approval, who did he tell you was responsible for it?'

"The wingless angel smiled gently. 'He told me it was his project.'

"'Thank you, sir. Now, Saraquael: whose was *Love*?'

"'Mine. Mine and Carasel's. Perhaps more his than mine, but we worked on it together.'

"'You knew that Phanuel was claiming the credit for it?'

"'...Yes.'

"'And you permitted this?'

"'He — he promised us that he would give us a good project of our own to follow. He promised that if we said nothing we would be given more big projects — and he was true to his word. He gave us *Death*.'

"I turned back to Phanuel. 'Well?'

"'It is true that I claimed that *Love* was mine.'

"'But it was Carasel's. And Saraquael's.'

"'Yes.'

"'Their last project — before *Death*?'

"'Yes.'

"'That is all.'

"I walked over to the window, looked out at the silver spires, looked at the Dark. And I began to speak.

"'Carasel was a remarkable designer. If he had one failing, it was that he threw himself too deeply into his work.' I turned back to them. The angel Saraquael was shivering, and lights were flickering beneath his skin. 'Saraquael? Who did Carasel love? Who was his lover?'

"He stared at the floor. Then he stared up, proudly, aggressively. And he smiled.

"'I was.'

"'Do you want to tell me about it?'

"'No.' A shrug. 'But I suppose I must. Very well, then.

"'We worked together. And when we began to work on *Love*...we became lovers. It was his idea. We would go back to his cell, whenever we could snatch the time. There we touched each other, held each other, whispered endearments and protestations of eternal devotion. His welfare mattered more to me than my own. I existed for him. When I was alone I would repeat his name to myself, and think of nothing but him.

"'When I was with him...' He paused. He looked down. '...Nothing else mattered.'

"I walked to where Saraquael stood; lifted his chin with my hand, stared into his grey eyes. 'Then why did you kill him?'

"'Because he would no longer love me. When we started to work on *Death* he — he lost interest. He was no longer mine. He belonged to *Death*. And if I could not have him, then his new lover was welcome to him. I could not bear his presence — I could not endure to have him near me and to know that he felt nothing for me. That was what hurt the most. I thought...I hoped...that if he was gone then I would no longer care for him — that the pain would stop.

"'So I killed him; I stabbed him, and I threw his body from our window in the Hall of Being. But the pain has *not* stopped.' It was almost a wail.

"Saraquael reached up, removed my hand from his chin. 'Now what?'

"I felt my aspect begin to come upon me; felt my function possess me. I was no longer an individual — I was the Vengeance of the Lord.

"I moved close to Saraquael, and embraced him. I pressed my lips to his, forced my tongue into his mouth. We kissed. He closed his eyes.

"I felt it well up within me then: a burning, a brightness. From the corner of my eyes, I could see Lucifer and Phanuel averting their faces from my light; I could feel Zephkiel's stare. And my light became brighter and brighter, until it erupted — from my eyes, from my chest, from my fingers, from my lips: a white, searing fire.

"The white flames consumed Saraquael slowly, and he clung to me as he burned.

"Soon there was nothing left of him. Nothing at all.

"I felt the flame leave me. I returned to myself once more.

"Phanuel was sobbing. Lucifer was pale. Zephkiel sat in his chair, quietly watching me.

"I turned to Phanuel and Lucifer. 'You have seen the Vengeance of the Lord,' I told them. 'Let it act as a warning to you both.'

"Phanuel nodded. 'It has. Oh it has. I, I will be on my way, sir. I will return to my appointed post. If that is all right with you?'

"'Go.'

"He stumbled to the window, and plunged into the light, his wings beating furiously.

"Lucifer walked over to the place on the silver floor where Saraquael had once stood. He knelt, stared desperately at the floor as if he were trying to find some remnant of the angel I had destroyed: a fragment of ash, or bone, or charred feather; but there was nothing to find. Then he looked up at me.

"'That was not right,' he said. 'That was not just.' He was crying; wet tears ran down his face. Perhaps Saraquael was the first to love, but Lucifer was the first to shed tears. I will never forget that.

"I stared at him, impassively. 'It was justice. He killed another. He was killed in his turn. You called me to my function, and I performed it.'

"'But...he *loved*. He should have been forgiven. He should have been helped. He should not have been destroyed like that. That was *wrong*.'

"'It was His will.'

"Lucifer stood. 'Then perhaps His will is unjust. Perhaps the voices in the Darkness speak truly after all. How *can* this be right?'

"'It is right. It is His will. I merely performed my function.'

"He wiped away the tears, with the back of his hand. 'No,' he said, flatly. He shook his head, slowly, from side to side. Then he said, 'I must think on this. I will go now.'

"He walked to the window, stepped into the sky, and he was gone.

"Zephkiel and I were alone in his cell. I went over to his chair. He nodded at me. 'You have performed your function well, Raguel. Shouldn't you return to your cell, to wait until you are next needed?'"

The man on the bench turned towards me: his eyes sought mine. Until now it had seemed — for most of his narrative — that he was scarcely aware of me; he had stared ahead of himself, whispered his tale in little better than a monotone. Now it felt as if he had discovered me, and that he spoke to me alone, rather than to the air, or the City of Los Angeles. And he said:

"I knew that he was right. But I *couldn't* have left then — not even if I had wanted to. My aspect had not entirely left me; my function was not completely fulfilled. And then it fell into place; I saw the whole picture. And like Lucifer, I knelt. I touched my forehead to the silver floor. 'No, Lord,' I said. 'Not yet.'

"Zephkiel rose from his chair. 'Get up. It is not fitting for one angel to act in this way to another. It is not right. Get up!'

"I shook my head. 'Father, You are no angel,' I whispered.

"Zephkiel said nothing. For a moment my heart misgave within me. I was afraid. 'Father, I was charged to discover who was responsible for Carasel's death. And I do know.'

"'You have taken your vengeance, Raguel.'

"'*Your* vengeance, Lord.'

"And then He sighed, and sat down once more. 'Ah, little Raguel. The problem with creating things is that they perform so much better than one had ever planned. Shall I ask how you recognised me?'

"'I...I am not certain, Lord. You have no wings. You wait at the centre of the City, supervising the Creation directly. When I destroyed Saraquael, You did not look away. You know too many things. You...' I paused, and thought. 'No, I do not know how I know. As You say, You have created me well. But I only understood who You were and the meaning of the drama we had enacted here for You, when I saw Lucifer leave.'

"'What did you understand, child?'

"'Who killed Carasel. Or at least, who was pulling the strings. For example, who arranged for Carasel and Saraquael to work together on *Love*, knowing Carasel's tendency to involve himself too deeply in his work?'

"He was speaking to me gently, almost teasingly, as an adult would pretend to make conversation with a tiny child. 'Why should anyone have "pulled the strings", Raguel?'

"'Because nothing occurs without reason; and all the reasons are Yours. You set Saraquael up: yes, he killed Carasel. But he killed Carasel so that *I* could destroy *him*.'

"'And were you wrong to destroy him?'

"I looked into His old, old eyes. 'It was my function. But I do not think it was just. I think perhaps it was needed that I destroy Saraquael, in order to demonstrate to Lucifer the Injustice of the Lord.'

"He smiled, then. 'And whatever reason would I have for doing that?'

"'I...I do not know. I do not understand — no more than I understand why You created the Dark, or the voices in the Darkness. But You did. You caused all this to occur.'

"He nodded. 'Yes. I did. Lucifer must brood on the unfairness of Saraquael's destruction. And that — amongst other things — will precipitate him into certain actions. Poor sweet Lucifer. His way will be the hardest of all my children; for there is a part he must play in the drama that is to come, and it is a grand role.'

"I remained kneeling in front of the Creator of All Things.

"'What will you do now, Raguel?' He asked me.

"'I must return to my cell. My function is now fulfilled. I have taken vengeance, and I have revealed the perpetrator. That is enough. But — Lord?'

"'Yes, child.'

"'I feel dirty. I feel tarnished. I feel befouled. Perhaps it is true that all that happens is in accordance with Your will, and thus it is good. But sometimes You leave blood on Your instruments.'

"He nodded, as if He agreed with me. 'If you wish, Raguel, you may forget all this. All that has happened this day.' And then He said, 'However, you will not be able to speak of this to any other angels, whether you choose to remember it or not.'

"'I will remember it.'

"'It is your choice. But sometimes you will find it is easier by far not to remember. Forgetfulness can sometimes bring freedom, of a sort. Now, if you do not mind,' He reached down, took a file from a stack on the floor, opened it, ' — there is work I should be getting on with.'

"I stood up and walked to the window. I hoped He would call me back, explain every detail of His plan to me, somehow make it all better. But He said nothing, and I left His Presence without ever looking back."

The man was silent, then. And he remained silent — I couldn't even hear him breathing — for so long that I began to get nervous, thinking that perhaps he had fallen asleep, or died.

Then he stood up.

"There you go, pal. That's your story. Do you think it was worth a couple of cigarettes and a book of matches?" He asked the question as if it was important to him, without irony.

"Yes," I told him. "Yes. It was. But what happened next? How did you...I mean, if..." I trailed off.

It was dark on the street, now, at the edge of daybreak. One by one the streetlights had begun to flicker out, and he was silhouetted against the glow of the dawn sky. He thrust his hands into his pockets. "What happened? I left home, and I lost my way, and these days home's a long way back. Sometimes you do things you regret, but there's nothing you can do about them. Times change. Doors close behind you. You move on. You know?

"Eventually I wound up here. They used to say no-one's ever originally from LA. True as Hell in my case."

And then, before I could understand what he was doing, he leaned down and kissed me, gently, on the cheek. His stubble was rough and prickly, but his breath was surprisingly sweet. He whispered into my ear: "I never fell. I don't care what they say. I'm still doing my job, as I see it."

My cheek burned where his lips had touched it.

He straightened up. "But I still want to go home."

The man walked away down the darkened street, and I sat on the bench and watched him go. I felt like he had taken something from me, although I could no longer remember what. And I felt like something had been left in its place — absolution, perhaps, or innocence, although of what, or from what, I could no longer say.

An image from somewhere: a scribbled drawing, of two angels in flight above a perfect city; and over the image a child's perfect handprint, which stains the white paper blood-red. It came into my head unbidden, and I no longer know what it meant.

I stood up.

It was too dark to see the face of my watch, but I knew I would get no sleep that day. I walked back to the place I was staying, to the house by the stunted palm tree, to wash myself, and to wait. I thought about angels, and about Tink; and I wondered whether love and death went hand in hand.

The next day the planes to England were flying again.

I felt strange — lack of sleep had forced me into that miserable state in which everything seems flat and of equal importance; when nothing matters, and in which reality seems scraped thin and threadbare. The taxi journey to the airport was a nightmare. I was hot, and tired, and testy. I wore a T-shirt in the LA heat; my coat was packed at the bottom of my luggage, where it had been for the entire stay.

The aeroplane was crowded, but I didn't care.

The stewardess walked down the aisle with a rack of newspapers: the *Herald Tribune, USA Today,* and the *LA Times.* I took a copy of the *Times,* but the words left my head as my eyes scanned over them. Nothing that I read remained with me. No, I lie: somewhere in the back of the paper was a report of a triple murder: two women, and a small child. No names were given, and I do not know why the report should have registered as it did.

Soon I fell asleep. I dreamed about fucking Tink, while blood ran sluggishly from her closed eyes and lips. The blood was cold and viscous and clammy, and I awoke chilled by the plane's air-conditioning, with an unpleasant taste in my mouth. My tongue and lips were dry. I looked out of the scratched oval window, stared down at the clouds, and it occurred to me then (not for the first time) that the clouds were in actuality another land, where everyone knew just what they were looking for and how to get back where they started from.

Staring down at the clouds is one of the things I have always liked best about flying. That, and the proximity one feels to one's death.

I wrapped myself in the thin aircraft blanket, and slept some more, but if further dreams came then they made no impression upon me.

A blizzard blew up shortly after the plane landed in England, knocking out the airport's power supply. I was alone in an airport elevator at the time, and it went dark and jammed between floors. A dim emergency light flickered on. I pressed the crimson alarm button until the batteries ran down and it ceased to sound; then I shivered in my LA T-shirt, in the corner of my little silver room. I watched my breath steam in the air, and I hugged myself for warmth.

There wasn't anything in there except me; but even so, I felt safe, and secure. Soon someone would come and force open the doors. Eventually somebody would let me out; and I knew that I would soon be home.